The Rest of My Heart

by Ronno

Adult Readers Only

THE REST OF MY HEART

Published by Bewere Books
Flagstaff, Arizona
https://www.bewere.net

ISBN: 978-1-62475-285-8
Printed in the United States, United Kingdom, or Australia
First trade paperback edition: February 2026

Cover and Interior art by Wiss
Edited by C.L. Methvin, Vincenzo Pasquarella, & Domus Vocis

For my parents

Thank you for giving me the kind of love that made it safe to find my own.

Mom, your strength and kindness have been a guiding light in my life. You always taught me to love without limits, to see the good in others, and to lead with empathy. You showed me that compassion is not weakness—it's courage.

Dad, your steadfastness and quiet integrity grounded me. You stood up for what was right, even when it wasn't easy, and because of that, I learned how to stand up for myself.

This story exists because of you both—because you created a home where I never had to hide, where being different was never something to fear.

Without you, I might never have believed that someone like Ryan could find peace, or that someone like me could find joy in simply being who I am.

With all my love and endless gratitude.

For my love

You are the heart of this story.

Jamie exists because of you—because of your quiet strength, your patience, your laughter, and your gentle way of holding all the pieces of me, even the ones I thought were too broken to be loved.

*Without you, this book wouldn't have been written. Without you, I wouldn't have found the courage to tell this story—to believe that someone like me could deserve something as beautiful as *us*.*

Thank you for showing me what true love feels like. For loving me, even with all the damage, the doubt, the healing still in progress.

You make the hard things softer, and the good things better.

This is for you. Kairo. Always.

For my friends—my chosen family

Thank you for welcoming me with open arms, wagging tails, and hearts full of love.

*You showed me what it means to truly belong. In a world that often asked me to hide, you gave me space to be seen. You cheered for me, believed in me, and reminded me that dreams aren't just for someday—they're for *now*.*

*Because of you, I learned how to laugh louder, love deeper, and live more fully as my *whole self*. You taught me that being different is something to celebrate, not fear.*

This story was born in the warmth of your friendship, your late-night conversations, your creativity, and your constant encouragement.

A special thank you to my best friend, Panic. You've stood by me through the darkest nights and celebrated with me in the brightest moments. Your presence has been a constant comfort and a source of light. I don't say this lightly—you are one of the most extraordinary people I've ever known, and I will cherish you always.

Thank you for reminding me that I never have to walk alone.

This one's for you—tails high, hearts open, always.

Chapter 1

It was cold in Ryan's room. A shiver traveled under the covers as he sighed and stared at the ceiling fan spinning lazily above him. The clock on the nightstand read 4:00 a.m.

"Great. Another night of no sleep," he muttered.

It had been months since Ryan had experienced a decent night's rest, and the exhaustion was catching up to him. Ryan sat up, the covers shifting as he scooted to the edge of the bed, inadvertently knocking over a half-eaten bag of chips he'd forgotten.

"Fuck, fuck, fuck!" he cursed, scrambling to stop the rest of the crumbs from spilling. He hastily shoved the remaining chips into his muzzle, cheeks puffed out as he crunched. Crumbs scattered across the bed and floor, furthering the mess.

Ryan was a striking blend of striped hyena and golden retriever, his appearance as unique as his personality. His build was impressive—broad shoulders and a powerful, athletic frame softened by the approachable warmth he exuded. Every inch of him seemed carefully sculpted, with well-defined muscles that spoke of quiet strength rather than pretentious vanity.

His coat was a masterpiece of texture and pattern. The golden retriever side gifted him a rich, golden-tan base, soft and thick while the striped hyena's influence painted dark, dramatic stripes across his arms, legs, and back, creating a wild yet elegant look. Along his neck and shoulders, his fur grew longer and slightly shaggier, giving him a natural mane that accentuated his regal presence. The spots of a typical hyena were darkest there, framing his face like nature's own touch of artistry.

His facial features were a harmonious balance of the two species. He had a strong, tapered muzzle that held both the softness of a retriever and the sharpness of a hyena's more angular structure. His blue eyes shimmered with a kindness that made him approachable, though the playful flicker of mischief in his gaze hinted at the hyena's wilder side. His semi- rounded hyena ears stood tall and expressive, often swiveling to catch every sound, while his tail—a thick, bushy plume—was golden with subtle streaks of darker fur running along the length.

Adjusting his disheveled underwear, Ryan swung his legs over the side of the bed. His bedroom was cozy and minimalistic, with soft gray bedding that was slightly rumpled from a rushed morning. A navy throw blanket was draped haphazardly across the bed, and the nightstand held a half-empty glass of water, a charging phone, and a small lamp with a warm glow. A neatly folded pile of laundry sat atop a sleek dresser, waiting to be put away, while a couple of worn sneakers peeked out from beneath the bed.

He sighed and trudged to the kitchen. He tossed the empty chip bag into the cupboard, letting out a heavy yawn as he grabbed the coffee grounds and filters.

Three months had passed since his breakup with Chloe, his girlfriend of seven years. The one-bedroom apartment still carried her presence; stray items left behind, faint memories clinging to every corner. As much as Ryan wanted to believe he'd been fine on his own, the loneliness was undeniable. And, if he was being honest with himself, it sucked. He sighed and trudged to the kitchen.

Ryan's apartment had the bones of a stylish and cozy home but was clearly reflecting the effects of neglect. The living room boasted a sleek gray sectional couch that wrapped around a low, modern coffee table with a glass top. Scattered on the table were a few empty coffee mugs, a couple of unopened envelopes, and a remote control that always seemed to be just out of place. A plush area rug softened the hardwood floors, though a few crumbs hinted at late-night snacks had while forcing time to pass in front of the wall-mounted TV.

The walls were painted in calming neutral tones, adorned with framed art prints of abstract designs and a couple candid photos from vacations long past. A potted snake plant stood valiantly in one corner, though its slightly drooping leaves suggested it was overdue for a drink.

The kitchen was compact but updated, with shiny stainless steel appliances and crisp white cabinetry. The sink held a small stack of plates and utensils, while the counter was dotted with a forgotten cutting board, a jar of peanut butter left open, and a half-full coffee maker that still smelled faintly of the morning brew. A fruit bowl sat on the island, with a single browning banana standing among the fresher apples. He tossed the empty chip bag into the cupboard, letting out a heavy yawn as he grabbed the coffee grounds and filters.

Despite the light clutter, the apartment gave off a sense of warmth and personality. It was clear that someone with a good eye for design lived there, even if they didn't always have the time—or energy—to keep it spotless.

Pulling a mug from the nearby shelf, his hand hesitated as he grabbed one with a picture of the two of them printed on it. The image was of them smiling in a sea of autumn leaves, carefree and happy. A pang struck his chest as tears welled in his eyes, streaking down his face and splashing onto the mug. The memory of that day resurfaced, vivid and painful.

Ryan stared at his reflection in the bathroom mirror, the faint sound of music Chloe used to play in the mornings drifting from beneath the door. Blinking slowly, he focused on his face, the voices in his head growing louder.

"You're a liar."

"You're just dragging out this pain."

And the most persistent: "You're gay."

His chest tightened, his hands trembling slightly as he gripped the sink. Ryan had grown up in a deeply religious household, where being gay was considered shameful—a "problem" that could be cured. Chloe had been part of that world, too. They'd met years ago at church, and everyone had said she was perfect: beautiful, driven, a talented singer, and stunning in every way.

For Ryan, she had seemed like the solution to his "problem."

Seven years ago, he'd asked her out, convincing himself that this was the right path—the "normal" life he was supposed to lead. At first, it was easy to ignore the feelings he'd buried deep inside. They shared laughter, chemistry, and dreams of a future together. They had talked about everything: raising a big family, rescuing dogs, and taking long vacations. For a while, Ryan believed he could live that life and silence the part of himself he was so afraid of.

But over time, the cracks began to show. Arguments over small things turned into days of icy silence. Ryan, ever the peacemaker, often apologized just to avoid conflict, while Chloe's stubbornness and headstrong nature made it harder to connect. Meanwhile, Ryan's feelings for men grew stronger, clawing their way to the surface no matter how hard he tried to suppress them.

At work, Ryan found himself drawn to the LGBTQ+ community in ways he hadn't expected. The nursing field was filled with people who were openly themselves, and it made him feel both comforted and envious. Here, Ryan found himself constantly wagging with an energy he couldn't quite contain. His posture was relaxed and confident, and he carried himself with an effortless ease that put others at ease too. Whether he was laughing with friends, running a hand through the soft fur on his neck, or flashing a grin that was equal parts charm and mischief, Ryan was the kind of presence that demanded attention—not through force, but through the natural, undeniable pull of someone who was warm and inviting.

One of his closest friends, Sam, was a nurse in the ER. Ryan had met him while filling in for the department one day.

Sam was a striking jackal with a broad, well-built frame that leaned toward the heavier side, giving him a sturdy and grounded presence. His coat was a rich blend of deep russet brown and sandy gold, with darker black markings accentuating the tips of his ears, muzzle, and tail. The sandy tones framed his chest and underbelly, softening his otherwise rugged appearance.

His fur was short but thick, with a healthy sheen that caught the light in all the right ways, and his angular, long jackal ears stood tall and expressive, often swiveling to catch the sounds around him. His warm amber eyes glowed with kindness, contrasting against the darker mask of fur surrounding them, and his muzzle was broad yet soft, hinting at his ever-present, gentle smile.

Sam's paws were large, matching his solid build, and his tail, full and slightly bushy, swayed naturally behind him. Though his appearance was undoubtedly strong, the soft curves of his heavier frame and the approachable warmth in his expression made him look as kind and inviting as he was.

Sam had a way of noticing when someone was struggling.

"Looks like you're about to make a big mess!" Sam had teased one day, tapping Ryan on the shoulder as he struggled to prep IV fluids.

Ryan glanced over and chuckled. "Oh yeah? And why's that, Mr. Genius?"

Sam smirked, reaching over and flipping the IV bag in Ryan's hands. "It helps if you hold it the right way." He pierced the bag with ease, handing it back to Ryan.

Ryan rolled his eyes, trying to hide his blush. "Ah, makes sense," he muttered sarcastically.

"You're really just coasting on those good looks, aren't you?" Sam teased, flashing a playful wink.

Ryan felt his face heat up. "What?! That's not fair!" he protested, laughing nervously as Sam sauntered off with an exaggerated shrug.

Did Sam just call me good-looking? The thought lingered in Ryan's mind, a small smile tugging at his lips before fading quickly. He forced himself to shake it off, reminding himself that it was wrong to think like that about another man.

But as the weeks went on, Ryan found himself floating to the ER more and more—and Sam was always there, conveniently working at the computer beside him. They chatted constantly, their banter attracting the attention of other staff. Ryan, quick-witted and comedic, often had the whole department laughing. Sam was always there to chime in with his innuendos and playful nudges, making Ryan's heart race in ways he couldn't ignore.

One day, during a quiet moment, Sam shared a bit about his personal life.

"Yeah, my last relationship ended last summer," Sam said, his smile faltering briefly. "He and I just didn't make sense. He wanted to stay in and binge awful reality TV, while I wanted to go out and dance—or at least goof off at a bar."

Ryan hesitated, unsure of what to say. "I mean, I'm not gay, but I can see how being with someone so different could be hard," he said, nervously fidgeting with his hands.

Sam raised an eyebrow, smirking. "Not gay...yet," he quipped, shooting Ryan a mischievous side-eye.

Ryan's cheeks flushed bright red. "I, uh, gotta pee," he stammered, shooting up from his chair and rushing out before Sam could respond. Sam raised an eyebrow and chuckled to himself, "That dude is so fucking cute".

Later that day the ER was in full swing, the air filled with the rhythmic beeping of monitors and the hum of chatter. Ryan was at the nurses' station, charting on a computer, when Sam appeared beside him with a devilish grin.

"Well, look who's working hard for once," Sam teased, leaning casually against the counter.

Ryan didn't look up. "That's rich coming from you, Mr. Coffee Break."

Sam feigned offense, placing a hand over his chest. "Excuse you! I was hydrating. Self-care is essential in this line of work."

"You're a hero," Ryan deadpanned, earning a laugh from a nearby nurse.

Sam leaned closer, smirking. "Don't think I didn't notice you sneak that jello cup earlier. Pretty sure that's theft."

Ryan finally looked up, his eyes narrowing. "Oh, and I suppose you're going to report me to the jello authorities?"

Sam straightened up, putting on an overly serious expression. "Absolutely. This is a high crime. Punishable by...I don't know, maybe a mandatory coffee date with the nearest charming nurse."

Ryan's cheeks flushed, and he quickly turned back to his screen. "Bro, shut up! You always gotta make it weird."

"Maybe. But you're laughing. You don't have to hold back so much, you know?" Sam said, nudging Ryan's arm. This made Ryan look at him quizzically and red in the face.

Before Ryan could respond, one of their coworkers, Karen, strolled over, hands on her hips. "Alright, you two. Are you going to work, or are you just going to flirt all day?"

Ryan groaned, running a hand through his hair. "We're not flirting."

Karen raised an eyebrow, unimpressed. "Sure you're not. Anyway, someone tell me why Room Four keeps ringing the call bell every five seconds."

Sam grinned, jumping in. "Easy. They miss me already. I've got that effect on people."

Karen snorted. "Or maybe they just need a blanket."

Ryan added with a smirk, "Yeah, and they're probably tired of your bad jokes."

"Excuse you," Sam said, pretending to be offended. "You laugh at all my jokes."

"Not all of them," Ryan countered. "Just the ones that are funny."

The small group of nurses burst into laughter as Sam clutched his chest once more. "Wow. Betrayed. Right here in front of everyone."

"Keep it moving, Casanova," Karen said, rolling her eyes but smiling as she walked away. It was time to head home.

The door to Ryan's apartment creaked as he stepped inside, letting it close softly behind him. He set his bag down by the entryway and toed off his shoes, sighing heavily. The smell of leftover takeout lingered in the air, faint and stale. The dim lighting of the small space only made it feel emptier, quieter—too quiet.

His shift had been long, but Sam's voice echoed in his mind as if he were still there, leaning casually against the nurses' station.

"You don't have to hold back so much, you know."

Ryan rubbed the back of his neck, trying to shake the memory. He shouldn't dwell on it. Sam was just...friendly. That's all. Sure, he was charming, funny, and effortlessly kind, but that didn't mean anything. Not really.

And yet, Ryan couldn't help but smile, just a little.

"Seriously?" Chloe's voice snapped him back to reality.

Ryan looked up, startled to see her standing in the kitchen, arms crossed. She was wearing an oversized hoodie and leggings, her hair pulled back in a messy bun. She had nice curves and a full frame. Most men would dream to have a girl like her in their lives. But the usual spark in her hazel eyes was dim, replaced with irritation.

"Uh, hey," Ryan said cautiously, shrugging off his jacket and hanging it by the door. "What's up?"

"What's up?" she repeated, her tone sharp. "What's up is the fact that I've been home all day, and the sink is still full of dishes. You said you'd handle them last night, Ryan."

Ryan frowned, walking toward the kitchen. "I was going to get to them after work. It's been a long day."

"Oh, yeah, must've been so exhausting," Chloe shot back, her voice dripping with sarcasm. "Meanwhile, I've been picking up your slack for weeks now."

Ryan blinked, caught off guard. "What are you talking about? I've been working overtime. I haven't exactly had a lot of free time to sit around and—"

"And what?" Chloe cut him off, stepping closer. "And be an adult? It's not just about work, Ryan. You don't do anything around here anymore. The trash, the laundry, the dishes—it's like I'm living with a teenager."

Ryan's jaw tightened. "That's not fair."

"Isn't it?" Chloe countered. "Because from where I'm standing, it looks like you've just checked out. You come home, you eat, you sleep, and then you leave again. I feel like I'm invisible to you."

Her words hit him like a punch to the gut. Ryan opened his mouth to respond but hesitated, the guilt rising in his chest. She wasn't wrong—not entirely. He had been distant. But it wasn't because he didn't care.

"It's not like that," he said finally, his voice quieter now.

"Then what is it like, Ryan?" Chloe asked, her tone softening slightly but still filled with frustration. "Because I don't know what's going on with you anymore. You don't talk to me. You don't even try to fix things between us."

Ryan rubbed his temples, the tension in his head building. "I'm just...I'm tired, okay? Work has been crazy, and I'm doing the best I can. Can we not do this right now?"

Chloe let out a bitter laugh. "Of course. Because that's what you always do, isn't it? Avoid the conversation. Push it aside like it'll magically fix itself."

"That's not fair," Ryan repeated, his voice rising this time. "You think I don't feel the strain? You think I'm not trying?"

"Trying?" Chloe scoffed. "Ryan, trying means actually showing up for this relationship. It means putting in the effort. Lately, it feels like you don't even want to be here."

Ryan froze, her words cutting deeper than she realized. He didn't respond right away, and the silence that followed was deafening.

Chloe's expression shifted, her frustration giving way to something more vulnerable. "Do you even want to be here?" she asked softly, her voice barely above a whisper.

Ryan looked down, his hands clenching into fists at his sides. He wanted to say something—to reassure her, to tell her that everything would be fine. But the truth lodged itself in his throat, impossible to ignore.

"I...I don't know," he admitted finally, his voice cracking.

Chloe's face fell, and for a moment, neither of them spoke. The weight of his confession hung heavy in the air, suffocating.

"I can't keep doing this," Chloe said quietly, her voice trembling. "I can't keep waiting for you to figure out what you want. I deserve better than that, Ryan."

"I know," he whispered, his chest aching.

Chloe turned away, brushing past him as she walked toward the bedroom. "Then maybe you should figure it out."

Ryan stood there, frozen, as the sound of the bedroom door closing echoed through the apartment. He sank onto the couch, burying his face in his hands.

Sam's words played in his mind again, unbidden: "You don't have to hold back so much, you know."

The truth was, Ryan wasn't just holding back with Sam. He was holding back from himself, from everyone. And now, it was all starting to crumble.

A new day started, Ryan let out a sigh before closing his locker and rubbing the back of his scruffy neck. He started restocking supplies at the med cart when Sam wandered over, sliding in beside him.

"Hey, you're doing my job for me now?" Sam teased, bumping Ryan's hip lightly.

Ryan glanced at him with a grin. "Well, someone has to pick up your slack. You're too busy being charming, remember?"

Sam smirked, tilting his head. "Charming and self-aware. It's a package deal."

Ryan shook his head, laughing softly. "You're ridiculous."

"And yet, you're smiling," Sam shot back.

Ryan rolled his eyes, focusing on the cart. "Someone has to keep the morale up around here. Guess that's us."

Sam leaned against the counter, his tone turning slightly playful. "Oh, is that what we're doing? Keeping morale up? I thought you just liked having me around."

Ryan paused, his hands stilling as his heart skipped. He looked over at Sam, searching for a hint of seriousness in his eyes. But Sam's smirk stayed light, teasing.

"Don't flatter yourself," Ryan said, forcing a laugh to cover the nerves tightening in his chest.

"Too late," Sam quipped.

Their banter was interrupted as another nurse approached. "You two need your own sitcom. Seriously, the rest of us can't get anything done when you're on shift together."

Ryan raised an eyebrow, smirking. "Oh, come on. We're not that bad."

"Speak for yourself," Sam interjected, crossing his arms. "I'm a delight."

"You're something," Ryan said under his breath, earning a chuckle from the group.

As the nurse walked away, Sam leaned a little closer, his voice softening. "You know, we really do make a good team."

Ryan swallowed hard, his nerves flaring up again. "Yeah...I guess we do."

Sam gave him a knowing look but didn't push further. Instead, he patted Ryan's shoulder. "Alright, Mr. Perfect Hair. Back to saving lives."

Ryan watched him walk away, a mix of emotions swirling in his chest. He felt the familiar weight of his self-doubt pressing down on him. Sam was kind, funny, and easy to be around—but Ryan wasn't sure he was ready to confront what all of this meant.

As Ryan's shift came to an end, he made his way to his locker, ready to shed the uncomfortable scrubs. He yanked them off and tossed them into his locker, standing there in nothing but a pair of tight black briefs. The cool air in the break room chilled his skin as he tried to shake off the day, his mind already on what he could do to unwind.

A sudden whistle broke his train of thought.

"Woah, Ryan, those scrubs really don't do you justice," Sam's voice rang out, teasing but warm. He had a wide grin plastered across his face as he wagged his eyebrows in playful jest.

"Bro! What the fuck?!" Ryan yelped, flailing a little as he tried to cover his chest and crotch, awkwardly spinning around as if he was in some bad movie scene.

Sam's laughter boomed across the locker room, clearly

enjoying the reaction. He casually tossed his scrubs aside, beginning to strip down, while Ryan hurriedly grabbed his own clothes, trying to regain some semblance of composure.

As Ryan awkwardly pulled on his jeans, he couldn't help but steal a glance at Sam. The jackal was a sight to behold—his broad back and thick arms rippling with strength, his waistline a little rounder than most, but still undeniably strong. Ryan swallowed and forced himself to look away, trying to push down the discomfort building in his stomach. It was hard to ignore how appealing Sam looked, but the internal conflict was becoming unbearable.

Finally dressed, Ryan started to head for the door, but he paused, the weight of his earlier argument with Chloe coming rushing back. Her voice rang in his mind, accusing him of being lazy, of never doing enough. And then there were those words—you don't have to hold back so much, you know. They haunted him, a constant reminder that he was hiding who he truly was. He clenched his jaw but stayed quiet for a moment, caught in his own thoughts.

"Hey, Sam," Ryan called out, his voice quieter now, hesitating for just a beat. "You wanna go to the bar tonight? You know, it's been a long week...and you said your ex never wanted to go."

Sam shot him a playful glance, his grin widening at the mention of a bar night. "Yeah? You sure about that? You're not just offering me a drink to distract from your scrubs-induced embarrassment, are you?"

Ryan chuckled but then nodded. "No, seriously. I could use a drink, and you're the only guy I know around here who's up for it."

Sam raised an eyebrow, his smile softening as he could see something more in Ryan's tone. "You got it. Let's go. It'll be good to unwind."

The night at the bar was everything Ryan had hoped for.

The atmosphere was loud, the music upbeat, and the drinks flowed easily. He and Sam settled in, laughing over shared stories and more than a few inside jokes. Sam's warmth and easy charm seemed to bring out the best in him, making Ryan feel like he could forget about his worries for just a little while.

As the night wore on, both of them began feeling a little tipsy, and their conversation turned into a more relaxed, almost carefree rhythm. The usual mental boundaries Ryan kept so carefully constructed were starting to blur, and he found himself laughing more than he had in weeks. He couldn't help but notice how natural it felt to be around Sam, how comfortable it was to just...be himself.

Sam nudged him with an exaggerated grin as they both shared a laugh. "I gotta admit, Ryan, I don't think I've seen you this relaxed in a while."

Ryan smirked, a little more tipsy than usual. "Yeah, well, Chloe was never one for bars or stuff even close to this. I just feel stuck trying to please her, you know?" The alcohol helped Ryan release some of the feelings he had held in for so long.

"Sounds like you need someone who can keep up with you," Sam teased, his amber eyes glinting with something Ryan couldn't quite place.

Ryan felt his heart race a little at the subtle shift in Sam's tone. "Maybe I do," he replied, a little quieter this time, his mind swirling.

The rest of the night passed in a haze, but by the time they got back to Ryan's apartment, neither of them seemed ready to say goodbye just yet. Sam pulled into the parking lot and put the car in park, but neither of them moved. They just sat there, the air thick with unspoken words.

Ryan leaned back in his seat, still a little tipsy, but feeling the warm, electric tension between them. Sam's eyes were on him, steady and patient, like he was waiting for something, but what? Ryan felt his heart pounding in his chest as if he couldn't ignore it anymore—the pull, the closeness. Without thinking, he leaned in a little closer. Their faces were inches apart now, and everything in his body screamed to just do it.

Sam didn't pull away. Instead, his breath hitched just slightly, his lips parting as if he was anticipating something. Ryan's heart skipped a beat before, without warning, he closed the gap. Their lips met in a soft, brief kiss. It was slow and tentative at first, like they were both testing the waters, but the spark that ignited between them was undeniable. The feelings of excitement and guilt battled in his chest.

CHAPTER 2

WHEN they finally pulled away, the silence was deafening. Ryan's heart raced, his mind a storm of conflicting emotions. Sam's wide, searching eyes softened into a gentle smile, as if he wanted to reassure Ryan that everything was okay. But for Ryan, the kiss felt like both a long-overdue step forward and an unforgivable betrayal of everything he thought he was supposed to be.

Pushing himself away, Ryan opened his mouth to speak, but no words came. His eyes welled with tears as he turned sharply, fumbling with the car door handle.

"Ryan, wait, I'm sorry!" Sam's voice followed him, gentle but urgent, as Ryan stumbled out of the car and began walking quickly toward his apartment.

Sam hurried after him, grabbing for Ryan's arm. "Ryan, please—"

Ryan jerked his arm away, spinning to face him. Tears streamed freely down his face as he choked out, "This isn't right, Sam! This isn't who I'm supposed to be!" His voice cracked, filled with anguish, the weight of years of repression and self-doubt crashing down at once.

Sam stopped in his tracks, his expression stricken. For a moment, he didn't speak, just stood there watching Ryan unravel, his own emotions flickering between guilt and compassion. Then, slowly, he stepped closer and reached for Ryan's paw, gently taking it in both of his. Ryan didn't pull away this time, though his body trembled with tension. His eyes staring at the strong hands holding his.

"Ryan," Sam said softly, his voice steady but tender. "I'm so sorry if I crossed a line. That kiss...It meant something to me, but if it wasn't what you wanted, then I'll respect that. You don't have to feel this way just because of me."

Ryan sniffed and tried to wipe his face with his free hand, but the tears kept coming. "It's not just you, Sam. It's me—it's all of this. I've spent so long trying to be someone I'm not, and now...now I don't even know who I am anymore." His voice wavered as he looked at Sam, raw and vulnerable. "And Chloe...I'm lying to her too. I'm lying to everyone."

Sam's ears drooped, his warm amber eyes full of empathy. He gently squeezed Ryan's paw. "You're not lying, Ryan. You're trying to figure out who you are, and that's not wrong. It's scary as hell, I know. But you don't have to have all the answers right now."

Ryan shook his head, letting out a shaky breath. "I just...I feel so guilty. Like I'm failing her. Failing myself."

Sam stepped closer, wrapping his arms around Ryan in a firm but comforting hug. At first, Ryan stiffened, unsure of what to do, but then he let himself sink into the embrace, burying his face in Sam's shoulder as he let out a quiet sob.

"You're not failing, Ryan," Sam murmured, his voice low and soothing. "You're a person. You're allowed to feel confused. You're allowed to take your time. And I promise, whatever happens, I'll be here for you. We don't have to read too far into this and make it more than it has to be"

After a long moment, Ryan pulled back, his breathing still unsteady but his tears slowing. "Thanks," he whispered, his voice hoarse. "I just...I don't want anyone to know about this.

Not yet. I can't handle that."

Sam nodded, his expression understanding. "I get it. This stays between us, okay? No pressure, no expectations."

Ryan managed a faint smile, though the guilt still lingered in his chest. "Okay. Thanks, Sam."

Sam smiled back and gave Ryan's shoulder a reassuring squeeze before stepping back. "Get some rest, alright? We'll figure this out one step at a time."

Ryan nodded, watching as Sam walked back to his car, waved back at him, and drove away. As he stood there in the cool night air, Ryan felt the weight of his emotions settle over him again. He didn't know where this road would lead, but it seemed like that had always been the case.

Ryan stood outside the apartment door for a long moment after Sam drove away. His chest felt heavy, and his mind swirled with guilt, confusion, and the lingering warmth of Sam's hug. He swallowed hard, trying to steady himself as he unlocked the door and stepped inside.

The apartment was quiet except for the faint hum of the refrigerator. He slipped off his shoes and shut the door softly, careful not to make too much noise. His eyes scanned the room: the living area, still slightly cluttered from earlier, the throw blanket crumpled on the couch where Chloe had been watching TV, and the faint smell of her vanilla-scented candle that had long since burned out.

Ryan let out a shaky sigh as he leaned against the door, his thoughts spiraling. Tonight had crossed a line he never thought he'd even approach. That kiss—Sam's warm lips, the softness of the moment, the undeniable pull he felt—was everything he had suppressed for years. It was real, so real it scared him.

And yet...the image of Chloe flashed in his mind. Her bright smile, the way she used to hum to herself while folding laundry, the life they had built together, even if it felt like he had always been holding something back. He thought about the fight earlier, of her accusing him of being lazy, of not caring. The way her voice had cracked, full of frustration and hurt, even as he avoided looking her in the eye. She didn't deserve this. None of it.

Quietly, Ryan walked down the hall toward the bedroom. The door was slightly ajar, and he peeked inside. Chloe was lying on her side of the bed, her back turned toward him, her body rising and falling in the soft rhythm of sleep. The dim glow of the moonlight illuminated the room, casting a pale light over the bed they used to share so closely.

He stood there, staring at her. She looked so peaceful, her long hair draped over the pillow, her favorite fleece blanket pulled up around her shoulders. Ryan's chest tightened as an ache of guilt gnawed at him—guilt for lying to her, for hiding a part of himself he had never dared to acknowledge, and now for what had just happened with Sam.

He leaned against the doorframe, his mind racing. What was he doing? He had built a life with Chloe—tried to force himself to love her in the way she deserved. And he did love her, didn't he? But it was never enough. There was always something missing, something he couldn't bring himself to admit until now.

Ryan slid down the doorframe. He dropped his head into his hands, his fingers digging into the fur of his scalp as his mind replayed everything—the years with Chloe, the laughter, the fights, the silences, and now Sam. That kiss. The moment he had crossed an invisible line he had spent his entire life trying not to approach.

For the first time, he allowed himself to think about what life as a gay man might look like. No more pretending. No more lies. But also, no more Chloe. No more safety net. The thought terrified him. Could he really live that life? Could he face the world, face Chloe, and admit the truth?

He sat there for what felt like hours, staring into the dim

light of the hallway. Finally, he pushed himself up, his legs stiff and his heart heavy. Ryan stepped into the bedroom, careful not to wake Chloe, and sat down on the edge of the bed.

He watched her for a moment longer, the weight of his guilt pressing down on him. He reached out hesitantly, brushing a stray strand of hair from her face. She stirred slightly but didn't wake.

"I'm sorry," he whispered, his voice barely audible. He wasn't sure if he was apologizing to her, to himself, or to the life they had tried so hard to build. Ryan lay down on his side of the bed, staring at the ceiling as the night stretched on. His mind remained restless.

As Ryan's restless mind finally surrendered to sleep, his consciousness gave way to a vivid dream. He was sitting on the couch in his apartment, but it felt different—warmer, softer, as if the air itself held a kind of comforting weight. The clutter was gone, and the faint glow of a lamp bathed the room in golden light.

Sam was there, sitting beside him, his sturdy, well-built frame leaning casually against the armrest, one arm draped over the back of the couch. His presence filled the space effortlessly, his warmth radiating outward like a soft, inviting fire. The faint scent of musk and cologne lingered in the air, mingling with something subtly sweet—like cinnamon or caramel.

As the golden light of a dream enveloped him, Ryan felt the pull of something deeper, a need that gnawed at the edges of his restraint. Sam's amber eyes lingered on him, studying his face with a quiet intensity that sent shivers down Ryan's spine. The air between them thickened, electric and alive, as if every unspoken word, every glance, and every touch had built to this moment.

Sam shifted closer, his broad hand brushing along Ryan's thigh in a way that felt deliberate yet unhurried. The heat from Sam's touch seeped through the fabric, leaving trails of fire in its wake. Ryan swallowed hard, his breath hitching as Sam leaned in once more, whose voice was low and rumbling with intent.

"Let me take care of you, Ry," Sam murmured, his lips grazing Ryan's ear as he spoke, each word sending a pulse of heat down his spine.

Before Ryan could respond, Sam slid down from the couch with a grace that belied his size. He knelt between Ryan's legs, his hands steady but unyielding as they coaxed Ryan to lean back. The warmth in Sam's eyes han't faded; if anything, it had intensified, burning with an unmistakable desire tempered by patience.

Ryan's heart pounded as he watched Sam's every movement—the deliberate way he eased Ryan's legs apart, his hands firm and confident on Ryan's thighs, the way his lips quirked into a sly smile as his gaze flicked upward. It wasn't just the act; it was the way Sam looked at him, like Ryan was something precious, something to be savored.

Sam's paws moved with purpose, sliding along Ryan's hips and settling with a possessive grip that made him gasp. Ryan's breathing quickened, the anticipation building as Sam pressed a kiss to the inside of his thigh, his lips warm and soft against the sensitive fur there. Each kiss sent a jolt of electricity through Ryan, his fingers clutching at the couch cushions as Sam worked his way closer.

The first flick of Sam's tongue was tentative, testing, but the growl of approval that rumbled from Sam's chest made Ryan's head tip back, a low, breathy sound escaping his lips. Sam didn't rush—his movements were deliberate, calculated, each stroke and press designed to tease and unravel him.

Ryan's world narrowed to the sensation of Sam's mouth, the wet heat, the gentle scrape of teeth, the rhythm that had him arching into Sam's touch without thinking. Every nerve in his body felt alive, his thoughts dissolving into the haze of pleasure as Sam took his time, his grip tightening on Ryan's thighs whenever he moved too much.

"Relax," Sam murmured between movements, his voice rich with amusement and heat. "I've got you."

And he did. Sam's presence, his touch, the way he seemed to know exactly what Ryan needed—it consumed him, grounding him and sending him soaring all at once. Ryan's paws tangled in Sam's fur, his breaths coming in short, uneven gasps as he felt himself being pulled to the edge, every sensation magnified by the unrelenting care and precision Sam poured into him.

Time became meaningless, the golden light of the dream wrapping around them like a cocoon. When Ryan finally shattered, his body trembling, Sam didn't pull away. He stayed close, his touch gentle, grounding Ryan as he came back down, his breath ragged and his mind blissfully blank.

Sam rose slowly and settled back beside Ryan on the couch. His paw slid around Ryan's waist, pulling him into a warm, solid embrace. Sam's lips pressed against Ryan's temple, his breath still hot and steady, the faintest smile playing on his lips as he whispered, "See? I told you to stop holding back."

Ryan could only laugh softly, his chest rising and falling as he tried to catch his breath. For the first time in what felt like forever, he felt completely seen, completely wanted.

The dream began to shift again, the golden light dimming as the edges blurred. Ryan woke with a jolt, his heart pounding and his chest tight as the weight of his dream followed him into the waking world. The room was dark, save for the faint light creeping in through the blinds. He turned his head to see Chloe sitting up on her side of the bed, her arms crossed, her silhouette rigid and tense.

"You finally decided to come home," she said, her voice low and sharp, slicing through the silence.

Ryan blinked, disoriented, trying to shake off the vivid memory of Sam from his dream. "Chloe, I—"

"Don't," she interrupted, her tone cold. She turned her head slightly, the moonlight catching the anger in her eyes. "It's almost two in the morning, Ryan. You reek of alcohol, and you can't even bother to tell me where you've been? Do you even care anymore?"

"Where have I been? What are you even asking?" Ryan sat up, running a paw through his fur, his mind scrambling for an explanation that wouldn't worsen things. "I just...I needed some time to clear my head. Work was rough, and I went out with some coworkers for a bit. That's all."

"Clear your head?" Chloe scoffed, her voice rising. "You've been doing a lot of that lately. Meanwhile, I'm here—alone—trying to figure out why you don't even seem to want to be around me anymore. And now you're out drinking? Ryan, this isn't you!"

Her words hit harder than he expected, the truth of them digging into the guilt he was already drowning in. He couldn't look at her, his gaze fixed on the floor as he struggled to respond.

"I'm sorry," he murmured.

"Sorry?" Chloe's voice cracked, a mixture of frustration and pain. "Sorry doesn't fix this, Ryan. You've been distant for months. I've tried to be patient, tried to give you space, but I can't keep doing this. I feel like I'm living with a stranger."

Her words cut deep, and Ryan felt his chest tighten further. He wanted to tell her the truth, to explain the turmoil that had been eating away at him, but the words refused to come. How could he possibly tell her?

Chloe stood abruptly, grabbing a small bag from the corner of the room. She started tossing clothes into it, her movements quick and purposeful.

"What are you doing?" Ryan asked, his voice shaky.

"I'm leaving," she said flatly, not even pausing to look at him. "I'm going to stay with my mom for a bit. I can't be here right now, Ryan. I can't keep waiting for you to figure out whatever it is you're dealing with. You don't talk to me anymore, you shut me out, and now you're coming home in the middle of the night smelling like you've been out partying? I deserve better than this."

"Chloe, wait," Ryan said, standing and taking a hesitant step toward her. "It's not what you think. I'm just...I'm trying to figure some things out. Please don't go."

She froze for a moment, her back to him, her shoulders tense. "Figure some things out?" she repeated bitterly. "That's all you ever say. You don't let me in, Ryan. How am I supposed to help you when you won't even tell me what's wrong?"

Ryan opened his mouth, but the words caught in his throat. He wanted to tell her everything, to finally let it all out, but fear paralyzed him. Fear of her reaction, fear of what it would mean for their relationship, fear of losing the fragile life they had built together.

When he didn't respond, Chloe let out a hollow laugh, shaking her head. "That's what I thought," she said quietly.

She zipped up her bag and turned to face him, her expression a mixture of sadness and resolve. "I don't know what's going on with you, Ryan, but until you figure it out, I can't stay here. I love you, but I can't keep hurting like this."

Her words were a knife to his chest, and all he could do was stand there, frozen, as she brushed past him and headed for the door.

"Chloe..." he whispered, but she didn't stop.

The door clicked shut behind her, leaving Ryan alone in the silence of the apartment. He stood there for a long moment, staring at the empty space where she had just been, his mind racing and his heart aching.

The guilt was unbearable. He sank onto the edge of the bed, burying his face in his paws. His dream, the kiss, Chloe's words—all of it swirled in his mind, leaving him feeling more lost than ever.

The two weeks that followed were a blur of isolation and self-loathing for Ryan. The apartment, usually filled with the soft hum of Chloe's music or her voice, felt like a hollow shell now, amplifying every creak, every sigh, every thought that echoed in his mind.

His phone buzzed constantly at first—Sam's name flashing on the screen with calls and messages. Each one was ignored, the guilt twisting tighter in Ryan's chest every time.

Sam: "Hey, you okay? I haven't seen you at work."

Sam: "Ryan, I'm worried. Please just let me know you're alright."

Sam: "I'm here if you need to talk. I mean it."

Ryan read every message but couldn't bring himself to respond. How could he face Sam after what happened? After he let his guard down, let things cross a line he couldn't un-cross? The kiss, the spark that had ignited so briefly, terrified him. He couldn't go back to pretending he was someone else with Sam, but he also couldn't bring himself to face the truth.

His manager had called after he missed three shifts in a row. "Ryan, what's going on? You've never no-called, no-showed before. Are you sick? Do you need time off?" Ryan had mumbled something about not feeling well, but the truth was that the idea of walking into the hospital and seeing Sam—or anyone—made his stomach churn.

He stayed in the apartment, the blinds drawn, the place growing messier by the day. Dishes piled up in the sink, empty takeout containers scattered the counters, and the faint smell of stale chips lingered in the living room. The bed remained unmade, Chloe's side of it untouched, a painful reminder of her absence.

Ryan had tried calling her a few times, each call going straight to voicemail. "Chloe, it's me," he'd said on the first attempt, his voice trembling. "I'm sorry about everything. Please...just call me back." By the fifth attempt, his messages had grown shorter, more desperate. "Chloe, I need to talk to you. Please."

But she never responded.

One evening, Ryan sat on the couch, staring blankly at the TV. A show played in the background, but he couldn't focus on it. His mind kept drifting back to the kiss with Sam, the way it had felt so right in the moment and yet so wrong afterward. He remembered the warmth of Sam's body, the way his scent lingered in the car, the way his lips had felt soft yet firm against his own.

And then, just as quickly, he thought of Chloe—her smile, her laugh, the way she had always been there for him. The weight of his betrayal crushed him, leaving him feeling like a failure in every aspect of his life.

A knock at the door startled him out of his thoughts. For a moment, he hoped it was Chloe, but when he opened it, there was no one there. Just a delivery guy walking away, leaving a small bag of food on the doorstep. Ryan had forgotten he even ordered it.

As he sat back down with the food, his phone buzzed again. This time, it wasn't Sam. It was his mother. He stared at the screen for a moment before silencing the call and setting it down.

The world outside kept moving, but Ryan felt stuck in place, unable to move forward, unable to go back. The days bled together, one after the other, until even he felt so disconnected since Chloe left, since he'd kissed Sam, since he'd last felt like himself.

Ryan dragged himself out of bed that Monday, the pressure of the past two weeks pressing down on him. He couldn't avoid work any longer. His absence had likely raised eyebrows, and he needed to hold onto some semblance of normalcy.

The morning routine felt robotic: shower, clothes, keys. As he slipped on his scrubs, he caught his reflection in the mirror.

His fur looked duller than usual, his golden stripes seeming to fade into the muted gray of his hyena features. His eyes, sunken and weary, stared back at him.

When Ryan arrived at the hospital, he was greeted by an awkward silence from his coworkers. The usual banter and morning energy seemed muted around him, as though everyone could sense the storm cloud hanging over his head. He avoided eye contact, especially with Sam.

Sam, however, wasn't one to be ignored. When their paths inevitably crossed near the supply closet, Sam tried to break through the wall Ryan had built around himself.

"Ryan," Sam started, his tone warm but tinged with concern. "Hey, can we talk?"

Ryan's heart skipped a beat, but he kept his expression cold, his voice curt. "Not now, Sam. I've got a lot to catch up on."

"Ryan, come on," Sam said, stepping closer, his voice quieter. "I know you've been avoiding me, and I get it. But you don't have to do this. You don't have to shut me out."

Ryan clenched his jaw, refusing to meet Sam's eyes. "I'm not shutting you out. I'm just busy. Let it go, okay?"

Sam's face fell slightly, but he nodded, stepping back. "Alright, Ryan. But I'm here if you need me. You know that, right?"

Ryan didn't answer. He brushed past Sam and threw himself into his work, avoiding any further interaction. But the desperation of Sam's words lingered with him, tugging at the edges of his mind.

The drive home was quiet, the sound of the engine and the hum of the tires on the road filling the void. Ryan gripped the steering wheel tightly, his thoughts racing.

He thought about Sam, about how easy it was to talk to him, to laugh with him, to feel seen in a way he hadn't felt in years. The kiss replayed in his mind, the warmth of Sam's lips, the way his paw had gently held Ryan's face. It was intoxicating, and yet...terrifying.

Ryan glanced at the cross hanging from his rearview mirror, a relic of his childhood and his religious upbringing. It felt like it was staring back at him, a silent reminder of the life he was supposed to lead. The whispers from his past echoed in his mind: *You're a sinner. This is wrong. You'll never be accepted.*

Could he really do it? Could he come out, risk losing everything—his family, his friends, his sense of stability? Was being with Sam worth upending his entire life?

He thought about Chloe, about the life they had built together, even if it wasn't perfect. She had been his anchor for so long, the person who kept him grounded. And though their relationship had been strained, she was familiar, safe.

Before he realized it, Ryan found himself driving toward Chloe's mother's house. He parked down the street, his heart pounding in his chest. He hadn't seen her since she walked out, hadn't heard her voice, and the fear of what she might say gripped him.

After sitting in his car for what felt like an eternity, he finally worked up the courage to knock on the door. Chloe answered, her expression a mixture of surprise and guardedness.

"Ryan," she said, her voice steady but cool. "What are you doing here?"

"I needed to see you," he said, his voice trembling. "Chloe, I know I've been...distant. I know I've hurt you, and I'm so sorry. I just...I want another chance. Please."

Chloe stared at him for a long moment, her eyes searching his face. "Ryan, you can't just show up here and ask for a reset. That's not how this works. I need to know what's really going on with you. You've been so closed off, so...different. I can't be in a relationship where I feel like I'm the only one trying."

Ryan's throat tightened. He wanted to tell her the truth, to finally let her in, but the words wouldn't come. Instead, he reached for her hand, his voice breaking. "I know I've made mistakes, and I know I've let you down. But I want to do better, Chloe. I want to make this work."

Chloe hesitated, her eyes filled with both hurt and hope. Finally, she nodded slowly. "Alright, Ryan. But this is your last chance. You have to be honest with me—completely honest. I can't do this if you keep shutting me out."

Ryan nodded, though the guilt in his chest remained heavy. As he walked back to his car, he couldn't shake the feeling that he was walking away from something real with Sam—something that could have been beautiful. But the fear of stepping into the unknown was too much, and for now, the familiar path, however flawed, was the one he chose.

Ryan threw himself back into his routine, clinging to the familiarity of work like a lifeline. He convinced himself he had made the right choice in trying to fix things with Chloe. The echoes of his religious upbringing reassured him—or at least, he told himself they did. Every morning, he woke up, plastered a smile on his face, and went to work. He cracked jokes with his coworkers, stayed late to help with shifts, and avoided any conversation that could lead to Sam.

But no matter how hard he tried, he couldn't completely avoid him.

It was after one particularly grueling shift when Sam found him. Ryan was heading toward the parking lot, his duffle bag slung over his shoulder and his mind set on just going home to collapse.

"Ryan!"

The voice stopped him dead in his tracks, his stomach twisting in knots. He closed his eyes for a moment, hoping he'd misheard, but when he turned around, there Sam was, standing just a few feet away. The jackal's face was a storm of emotions—determination, pain, and the kind of heartbreak that only made Ryan's guilt grow heavier.

"Hey, Sam," Ryan said, his voice forced into a casual, neutral tone that didn't match the panic racing through his chest. "What's up?"

Sam took a step closer, his eyes searching Ryan's face. "Don't do that, Ryan. Don't act like this is normal, like everything's fine. We need to talk."

Ryan shifted uncomfortably, his ears pinning back as he glanced toward the parking lot, already plotting an escape route. "I don't think that's a good idea, Sam."

"No, it's not a good idea. It's necessary." Sam's voice wavered, the raw emotion breaking through. "Ryan, I don't know what's going on with you, but I know what happened between us wasn't just in my head. You felt it too—I *know* you did."

Ryan swallowed hard, his throat dry and tight as he tried to maintain his composure. "Sam, I—"

Sam stepped closer, his voice rising in desperation. "Do you have any idea how hard it was for me to open up to you? To let myself feel something real for someone again? And then you—you just kiss me, and now you're acting like it never happened?"

Ryan looked down, unable to meet Sam's tear-filled eyes. "It was a mistake," he said quietly, the words stabbing at his own chest even as he spoke them. "I wasn't thinking clearly. It didn't mean anything."

Sam's breath hitched, and he took a step back as if Ryan had slapped him. "You're lying," he said softly, his voice trembling. "I can see it all over your face. You're lying to me and to yourself."

"I'm not," Ryan said, his voice colder now, harsher. He had to shut this down before it spiraled out of control. "You're reading too much into it. I'm with Chloe. I love her, and I'm trying to make things work."

Sam let out a bitter, humorless laugh, shaking his head. "Trying to make things work?" he echoed. "Ryan, you're not trying to make anything work. You're just hiding. Hiding from who you are, from what you want, from—"

"Stop," Ryan snapped, his fists clenching at his sides. "You don't know anything about me. You don't know what I've been through or what's at stake."

Sam's ears drooped, and for a moment, his anger melted into sadness. "I know more than you think, Ryan," he said softly. "And I know that kiss wasn't a mistake. It was the first time you let yourself be honest—maybe the only time. And now you're throwing it away because you're too scared."

Ryan felt his composure cracking, his mask slipping, but he forced himself to stay firm. "This conversation is over," he said, his voice sharp and final. "I've made my choice, and it's not you."

Sam stared at him, his tears falling freely now, soaking into the fur on his cheeks. "I hope you find happiness, Ryan," he said, his voice barely above a whisper. "I really do. But I don't think you will if you keep lying to yourself."

Ryan couldn't bring himself to respond. He turned away and walked toward his car, his heart pounding and his chest tight. Every step felt like dragging himself through quicksand, but he didn't look back. He couldn't.

Ryan sat in his car, the door slamming shut behind him. His chest heaved as he gripped the steering wheel, his knuckles white against the dark leather. The moment he turned the key in the ignition, he froze, staring blankly at the dashboard. His reflection in the rearview mirror caught his eye—his face was pale, his ears drooped, and his tear-streaked fur looked like the portrait of a man on the verge of collapse.

His breathing quickened as the weight of the past few weeks crashed over him. The fight with Chloe. Sam's words. The kiss. The rejection. Everything he had buried deep, pretending it wasn't real, now roared in his ears like a tidal wave he couldn't outrun.

He slammed his fists against the steering wheel, a guttural growl escaping his throat. "Why?" he barked to no one, his voice cracking. "Why can't I just be normal? Why can't I just *fix* this?"

Ryan leaned forward, resting his head against the wheel, his whole body trembling. Tears streamed from his eyes as he whispered, his voice shaky and desperate, "God...please. Fix me. Please, I've been trying so hard. I've done everything you've asked. I've followed the rules. I've kept it all inside. I love Chloe. I *do*...don't I? I can be the man she needs me to be. I can be the man you made me to be. Just..."

He broke off, gasping for air as his sobs overtook him. "Please, take this away," he begged, clutching at his chest like he could rip the feelings out himself. "I've prayed so many times before. Why won't you listen? Why won't you *help me*?"

The silence in the car was deafening, save for his choked sobs and the occasional sniffle. He stared up at the ceiling, searching for some sign, some answer, some miracle. "I don't want this," he whispered, his voice hoarse and barely audible. "I don't want to be this way. I just want to be good. I just want to be enough."

But the silence persisted, leaving him alone with his anguish. Ryan's head dropped into his hands, his tears soaking into his fur as he cried harder than he had in years. Somewhere, deep down, he realized he wasn't just begging God to change him—he was begging for a way out of the constant pain of living a lie. But he was too afraid to admit that to himself, let alone to anyone else.

Minutes passed, or maybe hours. Eventually, his sobs quieted, leaving him hollow and exhausted. He took a shuddering breath, wiping at his face as he tried to collect himself. "I can't," he whispered to himself, the words breaking his heart all over again. "I just can't."

With trembling hands, he started the car and began driving home with no answers, no relief—only the crushing guilt and fear that refused to let him go. He had to find a way to move forward with his chosen life.

Chapter 3

THE next morning, Ryan went straight to his boss's office. His heart raced as he stood outside the door, but he couldn't stay in the same unit as Sam. He needed to get away, to put more distance between them.

"Ryan, what can I do for you?" his boss asked, looking up from her desk.

"I...I need to transfer," Ryan said, his voice firm despite the storm raging inside him.

"Transfer?" She frowned. "Why? You've been excelling in this unit."

"It's just...personal reasons," Ryan said, avoiding her gaze. "I think a change of scenery would be good for me."

His boss studied him for a moment before nodding. "Alright. I'll see what I can do. But are you sure this is what you want?"

Ryan nodded, his jaw clenched. "Yes, I'm sure."

As he walked out of the office, he felt a mix of relief and regret. He had made his choice, and now he would have to live with it. But deep down, he couldn't shake the feeling that he was running away—not just from Sam, but from himself.

Ryan sat in his car outside the apartment, staring at his

phone as the screen lit up with Sam's name. Another message. He'd been getting them regularly over the past couple of weeks, and every time his chest tightened with a mixture of longing and guilt.

This time, the message was simple: "Hey, I hope you're doing okay."

Ryan's thumb hovered over the notification, his heart pounding. He wanted to respond—God, he wanted to. But he couldn't. What would he even say? *"Sorry I kissed you and then pretended it didn't happen?"* Or maybe *"Sorry I felt something real for the first time in my life and then ran back to my cage?"*

He closed his eyes, gripping the steering wheel so hard his knuckles turned white. Sam's voice echoed in his mind: *"You're lying to yourself."* And he had been. Every day for months.

When the messages first started, they had been a lifeline, a small tether to the person who had made him feel alive. Sam's words were always kind, always warm, always so *him.* At first, Ryan had typed out responses late at night when Chloe was asleep, his heart racing as his fingers hovered over the send button. But he never pressed it. The guilt of even thinking about Sam while Chloe lay in bed next to him was too much to bear.

As the days dragged on, Ryan had stopped opening the messages altogether. He told himself it was better this way—that ignoring Sam was the only way to move forward, to make things work with Chloe. But the truth gnawed at him. Each unopened message felt like another crack in the fragile lie he had built around himself.

And now, as the screen lit up again, Ryan couldn't take it anymore. He swiped the message away, and before he could think twice, he opened his settings. His fingers trembled as he scrolled to Sam's contact and hit "Block."

The second he did it, the finality hit him like a punch to the gut. He stared at the screen, his chest tight, his stomach churning. Sam's name was gone now, replaced with an empty silence that mirrored the one growing inside him.

Ryan leaned back in the driver's seat, his eyes stinging with unshed tears. Blocking Sam didn't erase the memories. It didn't erase the way Sam's laugh had lit up his world, or the way his touch had felt like a promise of something better.

But it did something else. It created a wall—a barrier between Ryan and the life he could have had. The life he was too afraid to reach for.

As he sat there, staring at the dashboard, he whispered to himself, "This is for the best." But the words felt hollow, and the ache in his chest told him otherwise.

Over the next six months, Ryan and Chloe settled into a tentative rhythm that resembled stability, at least on the surface. After their reconciliation, Chloe seemed committed to rekindling their relationship, suggesting date nights, reorganizing the apartment to feel "fresh," and even attending couples' church events together. Ryan went along with it, throwing himself into the routines of their life as if the structure could erase the turmoil inside him. They laughed occasionally, reminisced about old memories, and found fleeting moments of connection, but deep down, Ryan knew something was missing.

It didn't take long for cracks to reappear in their fragile peace. Chloe became more critical of Ryan, her patience wearing thin as she found fault in everything he did. If he left dishes in the sink or forgot to take out the trash, she'd sigh and mutter, "Why can't you just be the man you're supposed to be?" Her comments grew sharper, cutting into his already fragile sense of self.

"You used to be so driven, Ryan," she'd say, her tone dripping with disappointment. "Now it's like you're just coasting through life. Where's the man I fell in love with?"

Ryan would apologize, promising to do better, but every word felt like an act, a script he had to follow. He avoided conflict where he could, retreating into himself as Chloe's expectations became more rigid. She wanted him to lead prayer at dinner, to be more assertive about their future, to take on more traditional roles in their relationship. But the more she pushed, the more Ryan felt like he was crumbling under the expectations of trying to live up to a version of himself that no longer existed—or maybe never had.

As the months passed, Sam's memory lingered like a ghost in Ryan's mind. At work, he carefully avoided conversations about Sam, even though the jackal's laughter still echoed faintly in the hallways. On his drives home, he caught himself glancing at places they had gone together—the bar where they had laughed over drinks, the coffee shop where they'd shared casual, easy conversations. He couldn't escape the way Sam had made him feel: light, free, *alive.*

Even in quiet moments with Chloe, Ryan found himself drifting. He'd look at her across the dinner table and feel the weight of everything unsaid, the truth he was too scared to admit. He remembered the warmth of Sam's touch, the spark of their kiss, and the way Sam's words had cut through his defenses. It wasn't just that Sam had made him feel wanted—it was that Sam had seen him, the real him, and accepted it without hesitation.

But Ryan couldn't let himself think too much about that. Every time those memories surfaced, he shoved them back down, focusing instead on Chloe's expectations and the life he had been taught to want. Yet the harder he tried to conform, the more suffocated he felt, and Chloe's increasing control only added to his sense of entrapment.

"Ryan, we're not getting any younger," she said one night, her voice sharp. "If you can't step up and be the man this relationship needs, maybe we need to rethink everything."

And so, Ryan kept going, living a life that felt increasingly hollow, caught between the expectations of others and the truth he couldn't bring himself to face.

Another month passed and it was clear things had not changed. The night was tense from the moment Ryan walked through the door. Chloe stood in the kitchen, arms crossed, glaring at him with a look that made his stomach churn. He'd barely stepped inside when she started in on him.

"You're late again," she said sharply, her voice cutting through the quiet apartment. "What is it this time? Another long drive? Or did you find someone else to waste your time with?"

Ryan sighed, setting his keys on the counter. "Chloe, I told you, I stayed late at work. There was a situation with a patient."

"There's *always* a situation, isn't there?" she snapped, slamming the cupboard door. "You're always somewhere else, Ryan. You come home, you barely look at me, and you act like I'm not even here! What is it? Are you cheating on me?"

Ryan froze, his breath catching in his throat. "What? No, Chloe, I would never—"

"Don't lie to me!" she shouted, stepping closer. Her voice was trembling, but her anger burned hot. "You're hiding something, I *know* you are. You've been distant for months, you barely touch me, and you're always lost in your own head. If it's not another woman, then what the hell is it?"

Ryan clenched his fists, his body rigid as he tried to stay calm. "It's not that, Chloe. Just drop it."

"No!" she barked, jabbing a finger toward his chest. "I'm tired of this! You think I don't see it? You think I don't feel it every single day? You're not here, Ryan. You're not *with me.* So if it's not another woman, then what the hell is it? What are you hiding from me?"

Ryan's breathing grew shallow, his chest tightening as the words piled on. She stepped closer, her voice rising as she continued to poke at him, her accusations growing louder and harsher.

"Tell me the truth!" she demanded, her face inches from his. "What's wrong with you? What are you hiding? What's so horrible that you can't even look me in the eye anymore?"

Ryan's composure snapped. Tears welled up in his eyes as he finally looked at her, his voice breaking as he cried out, "I'm gay!"

The room went silent. Chloe's mouth opened slightly, but no words came out. She stepped back, her face a mix of shock, anger, and disbelief. "No," she said softly, shaking her head as if trying to will his words away. "No, you're not. You can't be."

Ryan sobbed, his shoulders shaking as he covered his face with his hands. "I'm sorry," he choked out. "I'm so sorry, Chloe. I didn't want this. I didn't mean for this to happen."

Chloe's eyes filled with tears, but her expression hardened. "You're lying," she said, her voice trembling. "You're just trying to hurt me. You're not...you're not gay, Ryan."

"I am," he said, his voice quieter but steadier this time. He stepped forward, grabbing her hand gently, as if to ground himself. "I am. And I'm so sorry. I've been lying to myself, to you, to everyone. I thought I could make it work, but...I can't keep pretending."

She pulled her hand back like his touch had burned her, her face twisting in anguish. "You lied to me," she whispered, her voice breaking. "You let me think we had a future, that we were going to build a life together, and this whole time—"

"Chloe, please," Ryan begged, tears streaming down his face. "I didn't know how to tell you. I didn't want to hurt you. I thought...I thought I could be what you needed, but I can't."

Chloe took another step back, her tears falling freely now. "I can't do this," she said, her voice thick with emotion. "I can't even look at you right now."

She turned and grabbed her purse, heading for the door

without another word. Ryan followed her to the threshold, but he stopped himself from reaching out. "Chloe, please," he said again, his voice trembling.

She paused, her back to him, before finally speaking. "Don't." Her voice was cold now, all the warmth drained from it. "Just don't."

And with that, she walked out, leaving the door wide open behind her. Ryan stood there, staring into the empty hallway, the sound of her footsteps fading into the distance. She hadn't grabbed anything—no clothes, no keys, nothing. She had left, just like that, leaving Ryan alone with the irrevocable consequence of his truth.

Ryan couldn't bring himself to be there when Chloe's family came to collect her things. The thought of facing her father and brother, their judgmental stares and unspoken accusations, was too much to bear. Instead, he left a key under the mat and texted Chloe back after a week of silence.

"I won't be there when they come. The key's under the mat. Tell them to lock up when they're done."

She never responded.

On the day her family arrived, Ryan drove aimlessly around the city. The thought of them going through the apartment—the space that had been theirs—gnawed at him, but he couldn't bring himself to go back. He didn't even know what he'd say if he saw them. So he drove, letting the hum of the engine drown out the chaos in his mind.

By the time he returned, the sun was setting. The apartment was dark and eerily quiet when he stepped inside.

Gone were the shelves of books Chloe loved to organize and rearrange. Gone was the rug she insisted tied the whole living room together. The art she had picked out, the vase she always filled with fresh flowers—everything that made the apartment feel like her was gone.

Ryan flicked on the light and stood in the middle of the now-bare living room. His chest tightened as he took it all in, the emptiness stark and hollow. For a moment, grief swallowed him whole. He thought of all the times they had spent here together—the laughter, the fights, the quiet moments on the couch. It was like they had stripped away not just her belongings but pieces of his life as well.

But as he moved through the apartment, something shifted. The emptiness wasn't just loss. It was possibility. Without her things, the space felt lighter, more open.

Ryan ran a hand along the kitchen counter, a faint smile creeping onto his face. It was like the apartment was asking him, *"Who do you want to be now?"*

For the first time, he let himself imagine. A new couch, a bold painting on the wall, maybe a bookshelf for the novels he never admitted he loved. He thought of inviting people over—not out of obligation, but because he wanted to. He thought of being free to choose who he was and what his space looked like, without worrying about anyone else's approval.

The sadness didn't vanish, but as Ryan stood there in the quiet, it no longer felt suffocating. It felt like the first breath of fresh air after being underwater for too long.

This was his beginning, however uncertain and terrifying. And for the first time in a long time, he was ready to face it.

Ryan walked into the hospital the next morning with a mix of determination and nerves knotting his stomach. It had been months since he'd stepped foot into the emergency department, but today felt different. Lighter. He'd spent so much time denying who he was, running from himself, but now, standing on the brink of a new chapter, he felt a strange combination of fear and excitement.

After clocking in, Ryan headed straight to his manager's office. The door was cracked open, and he gave a polite knock before stepping inside.

"Ryan, what brings you here?" his manager asked, her brows raised in surprise.

"I, uh, wanted to talk about transferring back to the ER," Ryan said, his voice steady, though his palms felt clammy. "I think I'm ready. I miss it there, and I miss working with the team."

Her expression softened, and she nodded. "The ER could use you, no doubt about that. They've been stretched thin the last few months. I'll set up the transfer."

Relief washed over him, and he managed a small smile. "Thank you. And, um, is Sam still working there?"

His manager tilted her head, her expression shifting slightly. "Sam? Oh...you didn't hear?"

Ryan's stomach dropped. "Hear what?"

"He left about two months ago. Took a position at Mercy General," she said, leaning back in her chair. "Something about a fresh start and better hours. I thought you two were close?"

Ryan's heart sank. His mind reeled at the news. "Yeah...we were," he said quietly, though the weight of his own choices hit him like a ton of bricks. He'd blocked Sam. Shut him out completely. And now, when he was finally ready to be honest with himself—and with Sam—it was too late.

His manager gave him a sympathetic look. "I can still put in the transfer. You'll have plenty of familiar faces down there."

"Thanks," Ryan muttered, forcing a smile. He left her office feeling numb, walking down the hallway in a haze.

As he made his way to the breakroom, memories of Sam flooded his mind—the way he'd joked with the staff, how he'd always been so warm and genuine. The way his eyes lit up when he smiled, and how Ryan had felt safe, truly safe, in his presence.

Ryan leaned against the counter, running a hand through his hair. "You idiot," he muttered under his breath. All this time, he'd convinced himself that burying his feelings was the right choice. That pretending he didn't care about Sam would somehow fix everything. But all it had done was drive a wedge between them, one he wasn't sure could ever be repaired.

His fingers instinctively reached for his phone. Opening his contacts, he scrolled to Sam's name—only to remember it wasn't there. He'd deleted it when he blocked him.

Frustration bubbled in his chest as he opened his messages instead, scrolling back months and months to their last exchange. There it was: a simple text from Sam asking if he was okay, sent during the weeks Ryan had been ignoring him. Ryan hadn't even responded.

Heart pounding, Ryan reopened Sam's contact and unblocked his number. He stared at the screen for a moment before typing out a message:

Hey, Sam. I heard you're at Mercy now. I know it's been a long time, but...I'd really like to talk if you're willing. I owe you an apology. I owe you a lot, actually.

He hovered over the send button, his thumb trembling. Finally, he hit send and let out a shaky breath.

As he slipped his phone back into his pocket, Ryan knew he couldn't change the past. But maybe, just maybe, there was still a chance to fix the future.

The coffee shop hummed with quiet conversation as Ryan walked in, his ears folded slightly in nervous anticipation. He spotted Sam sitting near a window, his tall jackal frame relaxed as he scrolled on his phone, a coffee already in front of him. Sam's tail gave a small wag when he noticed Ryan approaching, but his expression was guarded.

"Hey," Sam said with a warm but tentative smile.

"Hey," Ryan replied, sliding into the seat across from him. His own tail betrayed his nerves, curling slightly against the chair. He took a deep breath, hands trembling slightly as they wrapped around the coffee cup in front of him.

For the next hour, Ryan let it all spill out. He told Sam about the last six months: Chloe's anger, the suffocating guilt he had carried, and the deep, nagging ache that grew every time he thought about Sam and what he had thrown away. His voice wavered as he finally said it aloud, for the first time to someone who mattered: "I'm gay, Sam. I've always known it, but I was too afraid to admit it. Too afraid to face what that would mean for my life." His ears pinned back as his words tumbled over one another. "But I'm not afraid anymore. I'm so sorry, Sam. I lied to you, I lied to myself, and I pushed away the one person who made me feel like I could be...me."

Tears welled in his eyes as he reached across the table, his paws trembling slightly as they rested over Sam's. His tail gave a hopeful, nervous wag. "I don't deserve forgiveness, but I need you to know how much you've meant to me. How much that kiss meant to me."

Sam's ears twitched, and he looked down at their paws, his own tail wagging faintly but with uncertainty. "Ryan," he started, his voice soft but steady, "I'm really glad you're finally able to be honest with yourself. I know how hard that must've been, and I'm proud of you." He hesitated, his golden eyes flicking up to meet Ryan's tear-filled gaze. "But...I need to tell you something."

Ryan's heart dropped at the change in Sam's tone. His tail stilled as Sam gently pulled his paws back. "After four months of not hearing from you, I thought it was time to move forward. I've started talking to someone new. It's still early, but he's...he's been kind. He's helped me feel like I could move on from the pain."

The words hit Ryan like a blow to the chest. His eyes a mixture of shock and hurt as he thought of the pain he caused Sam. He blinked, his ears drooping low as he forced a smile. "Oh. That's...that's great, Sam. I'm glad you found someone who makes you happy." His voice cracked slightly, but he managed to steady it.

Sam's brows furrowed as he watched Ryan's reaction, the flicker of pain on his face impossible to miss. "Ryan, I didn't tell you to hurt you. I just...I need to be honest, too."

Ryan nodded quickly, his tail swishing once weakly before curling under his chair. "No, I get it. You deserve to be happy. You really do." He tried to keep a brave face, but the ache in his chest felt unbearable. Imagining Sam laughing and sharing intimate moments teased his mind.

The two sat in silence for a moment, unspoken feelings lingering between them. Finally, Sam reached across the table again, his paw resting briefly over Ryan's. "You've made a huge step today, Ryan. Don't let this stop you from finding your own happiness. You're finally free to be who you are."

Ryan nodded, his throat too tight to speak. His tail gave a small, hesitant wag as he offered a shaky smile. The weight of Ryan's choices stabbing at his chest. "Thanks, Sam. For everything."

Sam smiled, a soft, bittersweet curve of his lips that held both warmth and something unspoken. Without a word, he stepped forward, and Ryan met him halfway.

Their embrace was quiet, heavy—not just with the weight of what had been said, but with everything that had gone *unsaid* for months. It was the kind of hug that said *goodbye* without needing the word.

Ryan clung to him just a little tighter than he meant to, as if holding on could turn back time, could rewrite all the missed chances, the quiet longing, the fear that kept him silent. Sam's arms were steady, gentle, full of a love that had softened over time—no longer burning, but still *there.*

When they finally pulled apart, Ryan lingered for a second longer, his paws brushing Sam's arms. His chest felt hollow and full all at once.

A tear welled in the corner of his eye, and he quickly wiped it away with the back of his paw, trying to force a smile that didn't quite reach his eyes.

"You really waited for me," Ryan said, his voice quiet, cracking just slightly. "And I made you wait too long."

Sam didn't respond with words—he didn't need to. He just gave a nod, kind and resolute, eyes shimmering not with regret, but with compassion.

Ryan took a deep breath, and though his heart ached, it also began—just a little—to let go.

As they parted ways outside the coffee shop, Ryan watched Sam walk away, his strong frame fading into the distance. Ryan stood there for a moment, his ears drooping as he let out a shaky sigh. For the first time in months, he felt the weight of what he had lost—and the uncertainty of what lay ahead.

Ryan sat in his apartment, the quiet ticking of the clock on the wall the only sound as he stared at the blank TV screen. His chest felt tight, a dull ache spreading through him as Sam's words echoed in his mind: "*You've made a huge step today, Ryan. Don't let this stop you from finding your own happiness.*"

He leaned back on the couch, his ears drooping as he rubbed his paws over his face. The thought of Sam with someone else made his stomach twist, but it wasn't just jealousy—it was regret. Regret for the time he had wasted, the opportunities he had let slip by, and the pain he had caused them both.

As the emotions built, he finally let them out, tears spilling down his cheeks. His body shook with quiet sobs as he let himself feel the full weight of his choices and the reality of what he had lost. He cried for Sam, for the man he had been too afraid to love openly, and for himself, still grappling with the fear of being truly seen.

After a while, the tears slowed, and Ryan sat there in the stillness, breathing deeply. He wiped his face with his sleeve, his tail curled tightly against his side. He couldn't change the past, but he could choose how to move forward. He could hold onto the pain, or he could do what Sam had said—find his own happiness, even if it didn't look the way he had hoped.

Picking up his phone, Ryan stared at the screen for a long time, his thumb hovering over Sam's contact. Finally, he started typing, his heart heavy but determined to set the right tone.

Hey, Sam. I just wanted to say thank you again for meeting with me today. It meant a lot to me, even if it wasn't easy to hear everything. I'm so happy for you, and I hope this guy treats you as well as you deserve. I'd really love to meet him someday, if that's okay. I know we can't go back to how things were, but I hope we can still be close friends. You've always been such an important part of my life.

He read over the message a few times, making small tweaks before finally hitting send. As soon as it was delivered, he set the phone down and exhaled shakily, his tail loosening slightly from its tight curl.

For the first time in months, Ryan allowed himself a small flicker of hope. It wasn't the outcome he had wanted, but maybe this was a step toward something better. Sam had found a way forward, and maybe, just maybe, Ryan could too.

Ryan's phone buzzed on the coffee table not long after he sent the message. He hesitated, staring at the screen as his heart pounded. Finally, he reached for it, swiping the notification open to see Sam's response.

"Hey, Ryan. Of course, I'd still love to be there for you. You've been through so much, and I'm proud of you for finally letting yourself be honest about who you are. It takes so much courage, and I hope you can see that. You'll always mean a lot to me, and I'd be happy to introduce you to him sometime—maybe it'll help show you that there's love and happiness out there waiting for you, too. Let's catch up again soon, okay?"

Ryan read the message a few times, his ears flicking as the words sank in. A faint smile tugged at the corners of his mouth, though his chest still felt heavy. Sam's kindness was like a balm, even if the reality of his new relationship still stung.

He typed a quick reply: *Thank you, Sam. That means a lot to me. Let me know when you're free to meet up again—I'd love to hear more about how things are going. And thanks for believing in me. I'm trying to see the good in all of this.*

As Ryan set the phone back down, he leaned into the cushions of his couch, his tail wagging faintly despite the ache in his chest. It wasn't the ending he'd once imagined, but maybe it wasn't an ending at all—just the beginning of a different kind of relationship with Sam and a new chapter in his own life. Once again wiping a tear from his wet and warm cheek, Ryan held onto hope.

Chapter 4

RYAN finally picked up the mug he and Chloe had once shared—a cheesy, sentimental relic from a time that now felt like someone else's life. He stared at it for a moment, guilt and shame pressing down on him. Then, with surprising relief, he tossed it into the trash. The sound of ceramic breaking as it hit the bottom felt like a release, a small but significant declaration of freedom.

He moved through the apartment with purpose, scanning every room for anything Chloe left that tethered him to the past. There was the picture frame of them smiling at a holiday party, the blanket she'd insisted on draping over the couch, the candle she had picked out that still lingered with the faint scent of lavender. One by one, he gathered these remnants, piling them into a box marked for donation or the dumpster.

This wasn't about erasing Chloe or pretending she hadn't been a part of his life. It was about reclaiming his space, his peace. These objects, once symbols of a love that he had fought so hard to maintain, felt suffocating—physical reminders of the person he'd pretended to be.

When he was done, the apartment felt lighter, as if the walls had been holding their breath and were finally able to exhale. He looked around at the open shelves and empty corners and felt an unexpected pang of excitement. This was a beginning. For the first time in what felt like forever, the space felt like his—not theirs, not anyone else's, but his. The absence of those objects wasn't a void; it was an invitation to fill it with things that reflected who he was now, not who he had tried to be.

With a small, resolute nod to himself, he grabbed his keys. "Time to start fresh," he muttered, stepping through the door to find what the world had waiting for him.

Over the next few months, Ryan began rebuilding his life—this time as himself, unfiltered and free of the shame he'd carried for so long. He dove headfirst into exploring what made him happy. On sunny mornings, he found himself trekking through local hiking trails, the earthy scent of pine and dirt grounding him in the present. At home, his evenings were filled with gaming marathons, his headset perched on his ears as he laughed with strangers who slowly turned into online friends. Music became a constant companion, each song feeling like a soundtrack to his self-discovery.

The gym, surprisingly, became his biggest escape. Bark Bell, a quirky but well-equipped gym near his apartment, turned into a second home. It was there that Ryan met Rudy, a stout, muscular white rabbit who always had a collection of pink band-aids stuck to random parts of his body. "They have strengthening properties," Rudy would say with a grin whenever someone asked, which got him the appropriate nickname 'Bandaid'." Bandaid had a larger-than-life personality, always cracking jokes and flexing dramatically after finishing a set.

Through Bandaid, Ryan met Lysander, a towering purple werewolf with piercing eyes, sharp features, and an intimidating physique. But what surprised Ryan the most about Lysander was how matter-of-fact and proper he was. Lysander would correct Bandaid's wild stories with deadpan accuracy, which always made the rabbit burst into laughter. Despite his serious demeanor, Lysander had a dry sense of humor that Ryan quickly grew to appreciate.

"Ryan, you've been slacking on chest day," Bandaid teased one evening, tossing a pink band-aid in Ryan's direction.

Ryan caught it with a chuckle, wiping sweat from his brow. "You keep telling me that, but I'm pretty sure I can bench more than you now."

"Oh, now it's on," Bandaid said, hopping onto a bench and flexing in front of a mirror.

Lysander shook his head, adjusting the weights on his barbell. "Ignore him, Ryan. His ego's as inflated as his biceps. Which, by the way, are still disproportionate to his legs."

The banter between the three quickly became the highlight of Ryan's week. It wasn't just about working out anymore; it was about connection. For the first time in years, Ryan felt like he belonged somewhere.

Outside the gym, he began further stepping out of his comfort zone. He joined a local LGBTQ+ gaming group and found himself laughing more than he had in years. He started saying "yes" to invitations to hang out after hikes or grab dinner with people he met through new hobbies. Slowly but surely, the version of Ryan who had been hidden for so long began to shed his skin.

Yet, every so often, a pang of longing for Sam would creep into his thoughts. It wasn't about regret anymore, but rather a bittersweet nostalgia for what could have been. Ryan reminded himself that this chapter wasn't about chasing the past—it was about carving out a future.

One evening, after a particularly long hike, Ryan sat on his balcony with a notebook in hand. He jotted down his goals and hopes.. For the first time in years, the blank page felt like an opportunity rather than a burden. And as he looked out at the city, he realized he wasn't the same person who had arrived here all those years ago.

The crisp morning air wrapped around Ryan, Lysander, and Bandaid as they made their way up the winding forest trail. The sun peeked through the trees, casting long, golden beams onto the dirt path. Ryan felt a rare peace, the steady rhythm of his boots on the soil, grounding him in the moment. Bandaid bounced ahead, his little white rabbit form oddly spry despite his stocky frame, while Lysander followed with a calm, measured stride, his piercing purple eyes scanning their surroundings.

"You've been getting faster on these hikes," Lysander noted, his proper tone tinged with approval. "Finally learning how to keep up, Ryan?"

Ryan chuckled, adjusting his backpack. "Yeah, yeah. I'm just trying to stay ahead of Bandaid before he makes fun of me again."

"I wouldn't call it making fun," Bandaid quipped, bounding onto a large rock. "I'd call it 'light motivational ribbing.'"

They all laughed, the sound of their camaraderie blending with the rustling leaves. But as they rounded a bend in the trail, Ryan stopped suddenly, his ears perking up. In the middle of the path sat a dog—a golden retriever mix with a soft, golden coat that seemed to glow in the sunlight. Its muzzle was streaked with white, a sign of its age, and its gentle brown eyes looked up at them with curiosity and kindness.

"Whoa," Bandaid said, hopping down from his rock. "Where did this guy come from?"

The dog wagged its tail, standing up slowly. It wasn't scared or defensive, just...calm. A worn collar rested around its neck, but there was no tag in sight. Ryan knelt down cautiously, holding out a hand. "Hey there, buddy," he said softly. "Where's your owner?"

The dog sniffed his hand, then gave it a small lick before pressing its head into Ryan's palm. Ryan's heart melted instantly. "You're a friendly one, huh?"

Lysander crouched beside him, inspecting the dog with a critical eye. "It doesn't look neglected. Someone must be looking for it. But...no tag."

"No one around either," Ryan said, glancing down the trail. He called out, "Hello? Anyone lose a dog?" His voice echoed through the woods, but there was no response.

"Maybe they wandered off or got separated," Bandaid said, his long ears twitching as he looked around. "But we can't just leave him here."

Ryan nodded, scratching behind the dog's ears. "No way I'm leaving him out here alone."

The dog's tail wagged harder, as if understanding that it had just been rescued. Ryan smiled and stood, the dog trotting close to his side. "Alright, buddy, looks like you're coming with me."

"Just like that?" Lysander asked, raising a skeptical brow. "It could have rabies, or even worse—canine parvovirus."

Ryan and Bandaid looked at each other both confused and slightly amused.

Ryan shrugged. "What else am I supposed to do? He's got no ID, no one's around...Besides, look at him." He gestured to the dog, who was now leaning against Ryan's leg, looking up at him with adoration. "He's a sweetheart."

Bandaid grinned. "I mean, it *is* the perfect cliché: the single guy rescues a dog and his life gets better instantly."

Ryan laughed, shaking his head. "Yeah, well, let's hope it's that simple."

As they finished the hike, the dog stayed at Ryan's side, matching his pace with surprising ease for its age. By the time they reached the parking lot, Ryan had already decided on a temporary name: Max.

When Ryan finally got home, Max followed him inside, sniffing every corner of the apartment. The golden retriever flopped down on the rug with a sigh, as though he'd always belonged there. Ryan smiled, feeling an unexpected warmth spread through him. The pattering of paws was a welcomed addition to the space.

Ryan did his best to take a photo of Max, though the dog seemed far more interested in wagging his tail and trying to nuzzle the phone than sitting still. After a few attempts, he managed to snap a decent shot of Max's golden face and warm, kind eyes. He printed a handful of flyers and spent his free afternoon walking around the neighborhood, pinning them to trees, light poles, and bulletin boards.

Max trotted happily beside him, his leash loose as if he knew he didn't need it. His sweet, doggy grin never wavered, even when Ryan felt the pangs of worry over whether someone would claim him. Despite knowing it was the right thing to do, part of him didn't want anyone to come forward. Max had already made himself at home, both in the apartment and in Ryan's heart.

By the time evening rolled around, Ryan was exhausted. He tossed his keys on the counter and slumped onto the couch, Max following close behind. The retriever hopped up beside him, resting his head on Ryan's lap with a soft sigh. Ryan absently scratched behind his ears, staring at the blank TV screen and letting his mind wander—something he'd been doing a lot lately.

That night, sleep didn't come easily. When it did, it brought with it the same haunting dream that had plagued Ryan on and off for years. In the dream, he was back in the church of his childhood, standing before a faceless congregation. Their voices rang out in disapproval, accusing him of being unworthy, sinful, broken. He tried to speak, to explain himself, but the words never came. Instead, he dropped to his knees, tears streaming down his face as he begged for forgiveness, for some-one—anyone—to fix him.

When he woke, his chest was tight, and his fur was damp with sweat. His breaths came in shallow, ragged gasps, and he clutched the sheets as though they could anchor him. Tears pricked at the corners of his eyes as the shame and fear from the dream lingered, weighing heavy on his heart.

A soft weight shifted at the foot of the bed, and before Ryan could process it, Max was there. The retriever climbed up onto the bed with surprising grace for his size, settling beside Ryan and resting his head gently on his chest.

Ryan froze, then let out a shaky breath. He felt the warmth of Max's body, the steady rise and fall of his breathing, and the soothing weight of his presence. Max looked up at him with those kind, brown eyes, full of unconditional love and understanding.

Ryan's tears spilled over, and he wrapped his arms around Max, burying his face in the dog's soft, golden fur. "I'm sorry, Max," he whispered. "I'm trying...I'm trying so hard."

Max didn't move, didn't pull away. He simply stayed there, a quiet, grounding presence that seemed to say, *You're okay. I'm here.*

For the first time in a long while, Ryan didn't feel alone. As his breathing slowed and his tears subsided, he let himself hold onto that small comfort, grateful for the dog who had found his way into his life—and, somehow, into the pieces of his heart he was still trying to mend. Ryan fell asleep and awoke with Max snoozing nudged between his legs, the best rest Ryan could recall having had in years.

The next morning, Ryan sat at his computer, Max curled up at his feet. The retriever's gentle snoring filled the quiet apartment as Ryan typed into Barkle, searching for nearby dog daycares and rescue organizations. He had grown attached to Max over the past day, but he still needed to do the responsible thing and see if anyone was looking for him.

When Bandaid and Lysander arrived at his door, Ryan quickly explained his plan. "There's a dog daycare a few blocks over and a rescue center not too far from that. I figured we could start there and see if anyone recognizes him."

Bandaid, munching on a protein bar, grinned. "Sounds good, though I'm calling it now—this dog's staying with you. He's clearly already claimed you."

Lysander raised an eyebrow. "It's admirable that Ryan is being diligent, though. One can never assume."

Ryan chuckled as they headed out, Max happily trotting alongside them. The retriever's tail wagged furiously, and he looked back at Ryan every so often, as if to make sure he was still there.

The first stop was uneventful, with the daycare staff saying they hadn't seen Max before. Ryan made his way to the Rescue Center, a modest brick building with a cheerful painted sign that read "Paws and Tails Rescue." As they stepped inside, a bell jingled, and a wave of cool air washed over them.

Ryan took in the clean, welcoming lobby. Behind the desk stood a shorter, well-built striped hyena. His brown eyes were framed by soft, fluffy bangs that fell slightly into his face, and his muscular legs and broader frame suggested years of running and physical activity. Despite his strong build, there was an air of quiet timidity about him, especially when he noticed the group enter.

"Hi, welcome to 'Paws and Tails'," he said, his voice soft but warm. His gaze flickered nervously between Ryan and his friends before landing on Max. "Oh, what a handsome boy!"

Ryan felt a sudden lump in his throat as their eyes met. The hyena's soft blush deepened, and Ryan immediately lost his train of thought. Max wagged his tail, oblivious to the tension in the room.

"I, uh..." Ryan stammered, struggling to find his words. Bandaid, ever the extrovert, nudged him with an elbow, smirking.

"He found this guy wandering around during a hike," Bandaid said, gesturing to Max. "We were hoping someone here might recognize him. Got a collar, but no tags."

The hyena—Jamie, according to the name tag pinned to his polo shirt—nodded, fiddling with a pen on the desk. "I haven't seen him before, but we could leave a poster up here and check with some of the other volunteers. Sometimes people in the community send in photos of lost dogs they're looking for."

Ryan finally managed to pull himself together enough to respond. "That would be great, thank you. I've got some flyers with me." He handed one over, their fingers brushing briefly. Jamie's blush deepened, and Ryan felt his own face heat up.

"You can count on me to ask around," Jamie said softly, his gaze darting to Ryan and then to Max. "I'll make sure it gets to everyone here."

"Thank you," Ryan said, his voice quieter than usual. His tail wagged slightly, betraying his swirl of emotions.

Jamie hesitated, then smiled faintly. "Good luck finding his owner. He seems like a really good dog."

Bandaid raised an eyebrow once they were outside. "So... what was that?"

"What was what?" Ryan asked, playing dumb, though his ears betrayed him by folding back slightly.

"Don't play coy," Lysander said, matter-of-factly. "You and the shy striped hyena. You both turned into nervous wrecks in there."

Ryan groaned, his face flushing. "I wasn't nervous."

"Sure, and Max isn't adorable," Bandaid teased, laughing.

As the trio strolled back toward Ryan's apartment, Max trotted ahead, his golden tail wagging like a metronome. Ryan couldn't shake the faint blush lingering on his cheeks, and unfortunately, Bandaid and Lysander weren't about to let him off the hook.

"So," Bandaid began, grinning like the mischievous rabbit he was, "are we just going to ignore the fact that you and Jamie were two sentences away from exchanging love poems in there?"

Ryan rolled his eyes, but his ears betrayed him again, folding back slightly. "It wasn't like that, you're nuts."

"Sure," Lysander said, his voice deadpan but his lips curling into a small smirk. "Because normal people blush so hard they practically glow."

"You're both ridiculous," Ryan shot back, trying to sound annoyed but failing as his tail gave a small wag. "It was just a quick conversation. I don't even know him."

"Doesn't matter," Bandaid said, hopping a little ahead and spinning to walk backward so he could face Ryan. "You're already crushing. I could see it all over your face. And Jamie? Dude couldn't stop blushing either. It was adorable."

Ryan sighed, trying to deflect. "Okay, fine. Maybe he was cute, but you two are one to talk."

"Excuse me?" Bandaid asked, raising a fluffy brow.

Ryan smirked, pointing a finger at them. Ryan attempted to redirect the conversation. "I'm not blind, you know. You two have been hanging out more and more. And don't think I haven't noticed the way you tease each other. It's borderline flirting at this point."

Lysander's ears perked, and he crossed his arms. "Flirting? That's absurd."

"Uh-huh," Ryan said, his grin widening. "Come on, Lysander. I saw you help Bandaid with his bench press the other day. You practically guided his arms like you were in some cheesy rom-com."

Bandaid snorted, trying and failing to suppress a laugh.

"Okay, that's fair, but in his defense, I asked for a spot!"

"Right," Ryan said, drawing out the word with exaggerated skepticism. "And the lingering hand on the shoulder? Just part of the workout routine?"

Now it was Lysander's turn to look slightly flustered, though he quickly composed himself. "I take physical safety very seriously."

Ryan laughed. "Sure you do, Mr. Romantic Spotter."

Bandaid chuckled, nudging Lysander with his elbow. "He's not wrong, though. We *have* been spending a lot of time together. Maybe we're just better friends than we thought."

Lysander cleared his throat, his ears flicking. "Perhaps."

Ryan smirked, feeling the tables turn in his favor. "Don't worry, I'm rooting for you two. Just let me know when I need to buy the wedding gift."

Bandaid barked out a laugh, his little pink bandaids catching the sunlight as he shook his head. "Oh, don't think this gets you off the hook, Romeo. You're still going back to that rescue center, right? Because if you don't, I will personally drag you there and hand-deliver your number to Jamie myself."

Ryan groaned but couldn't help smiling. "We'll see. For now, let's just get Max home before you two start planning my nonexistent wedding."

As the teasing died down, Ryan felt lighter, grateful for the friendship and support that surrounded him. Even if they loved to poke fun, Bandaid and Lysander had a knack for reminding him that new chapters, no matter how unexpected, were worth embracing.

Chapter 5

THE next morning, Ryan woke to the soft chime of his phone. Squinting against the sunlight streaming through his window, his eyes adjusted as he read the message.

Jamie: "*Hey! I may have a leash for you to check out!*"

Ryan blinked, a grin tugging at his lips as he typed back.

Ryan: "*A leash, huh?*"

A long pause followed before Jamie responded.

Jamie: "*Oh! Wait—leads! I meant a lead for Max. Not leash. Sorry. :D*"

Ryan laughed to himself, shaking his head.

Ryan: "*Relax, I'm just teasing. I'll swing by later with Max and see what you've got.*"

Jamie: "Okay. *See you later.*"

Later that day, Ryan leashed up Max and made his way to the rescue. The building was calm, the soft hum of music filtering through the quiet space. Ryan walked in and glanced around until he spotted Jamie in the back, kneeling by some shelving and organizing supplies.

Jamie was crouched over, focused on a stack of bags. His

shirt had lifted slightly, revealing a strip of golden-striped fur on his lower back and a sliver of dark blue waistband. There was a faint glimmer of sweat on his back, and Ryan felt his breath hitch before quickly looking away.

Jamie glanced back as if sensing Ryan's gaze, his soft brown eyes widening slightly. He immediately stood, tugging his shirt down in a flustered motion. "Oh! Uh hi, Ryan," he said, his voice soft and a little shaky. His ears tilted back slightly, and he avoided meeting Ryan's gaze directly.

"Hey, Jamie," Ryan replied, trying to sound casual despite the awkwardness. He cleared his throat and gestured to Max. "Thought I'd stop by and see what leads you've got."

Jamie nodded, brushing his hands on his pants before looking back at Max. "So, I've been thinking about it more," he began, his voice quiet but steady. "When older dogs go missing like this, it's usually connected to an older owner. I decided to check the paper's classifieds…just in case."

Ryan tilted his head, curious, as Jamie reached for a folded newspaper on the counter. "And?"

Jamie hesitated, his gaze lowering for a moment. "I, um…I think I found something." He opened the paper and handed it to Ryan, pointing to a small obituary. "There's a man named Richard—he passed away recently. Heart attack, in a park not far from here. And…" Jamie's voice softened as Ryan looked at the accompanying photo, "…that's Max."

The black-and-white photo was grainy, but there was no mistaking Max's golden coat and sweet, soulful face. He was sitting beside a kind-looking older wolf with gentle eyes and a wide smile.

Ryan felt his chest tighten. "Oh, man…" He stroked Max's head as the dog wagged his tail, oblivious to the seriousness of the moment.

"I did a little more digging," Jamie continued, his ears flicking nervously. "Richard doesn't have a ton of family left, but there's a number here for a niece. I thought you might want to call her and...you know, see if they're looking for Max."

Ryan nodded, his throat suddenly dry as he stared at the number Jamie had jotted down on a piece of paper. A mix of emotions churned inside him—relief at having a lead, sadness at the thought of giving Max up, and guilt at the selfish part of him that hoped no one would claim the dog.

Jamie noticed the conflicted look on Ryan's face and offered him a small, reassuring smile. "I know it's hard. You've bonded with him. But...if this is his family, he deserves to be with them."

Ryan looked down at Max, who was gazing up at him with pure trust. "Yeah, you're right," he said quietly, though his voice cracked slightly.

Jamie stepped a little closer, his tone softer now. "Hey, whatever happens, you've done something really good for Max. And if he does end up staying with you...well, I think he's pretty lucky."

Ryan managed a weak smile. "Thanks, Jamie. That...means more than you know."

Jamie nodded, his gaze lingering on Ryan for a moment before stepping back. "Let me know how it goes, okay?" Jamie looked away embarrassed and reddened. "Feel free to shoot me a text or just come by, I work all the time."

"Yeah," Ryan said, clutching the paper with the niece's number and wearing a blushed smile. "I will."

As Ryan left the rescue, Max trotting beside him, he couldn't help but glance back at Jamie. There was something about his quiet kindness that stuck with Ryan, even as his heart wrestled with the bittersweet reality ahead.

Ryan sat on the edge of his couch, Max lying next to him, his large frame sprawled out comfortably. He stared at the piece of paper Jamie had given him, the niece's number still fresh in his mind. With a deep breath, he dialed the number.

The phone rang a few times before a soft voice answered. "Hello?"

"Hi, is this Amanda?" Ryan asked, his voice a little shaky. "My name's Ryan, and I found your dog...well your uncle's dog, I should say."

There was a pause on the other end of the line. "Mac?" she repeated, a bit of urgency in her voice. "Oh my gosh, you found him? Is he okay?" Mac would explain why the name Max worked so effectively when he was called, Ryan thought.

"Yeah, I found him a few days ago," Ryan said, trying to keep his voice steady. "He's safe and sound. He's with me right now."

Amanda exhaled a breath of relief. "Oh, thank God. I've been so worried. I wasn't able to get back into town in time to search for him. I...I should've been there."

Ryan looked down at the dog beside him, scratching behind Max's ears. "He's been a good boy," Ryan said gently. "He's well-behaved and seems like he's been through a lot, but he's adjusting. You can tell he was well-loved."

"Yeah, that sounds like the Mac I remember," Amanda replied, her voice growing more subdued. "I'd say I can come pick him up but...I'm allergic to dogs, and I live pretty far from the city. I can't take him in at this moment. I'll ask around, see if any of my friends can help. Maybe I can arrange for some care until I figure something out." She seemed to be thinking out loud.

Ryan's heart dropped. He was already so attached to Max, and the thought of him leaving was unbearable. "I understand," Ryan said quietly, running his hand along Max's golden fur. "But, Amanda...if it's okay with you...I'd love to keep him, even if it's just until you find someone close to you to take care of him. I know it's a big request, but I promise I'll take care of him, and I'll give him the kind of life that Richard would've wanted for him."

There was a pause on the other end of the line, and Ryan's anxiety spiked. Finally, Amanda spoke, her voice soft but filled with gratitude. "My uncle loved that dog. If you went through all this trouble to just find his owner I can tell you truly care. If you promise to take care of him...then I'm okay with that. I know Mac deserves a good home, and it sounds like you're the right person for the job."

Relief washed over Ryan like a wave. He looked at Max, who had stretched out on the floor, his large body filling up the space with comfort. "Thank you so much, Amanda. I promise you, I'll love him like Richard did. He's going to have the best life I can give him."

Amanda's voice wavered as she spoke again. "I'm so grateful, Ryan. Thank you. You've made my day."

Ryan's heart swelled with emotion as he hung up the phone, and he turned to Max, who was now sitting up and giving him a curious glance. With a smile, Ryan got down on the floor beside him, gently scratching behind his ears.

"You're staying with me now, buddy," Ryan whispered, his voice thick with emotion. "I'm so sorry for everything you've been through, but I'll make sure you have the life you deserve. I'm going to take care of you, and you'll always have a home with me."

Max licked Ryan's face, his large tail thumping happily on the ground. Ryan laughed softly through the tears, feeling a warmth fill his chest. Max was more than just a dog to him now—he was family. "You're not going anywhere, Mac...or should I say Max," Ryan chuckled, rubbing the dog's belly as Max rolled over to show his soft underbelly. "I've got you now, and I'm never letting you go."

That night, after a long day of navigating all the emotions and surprises regarding Max, Ryan found himself sitting with Bandaid and Lysander, sharing pizza and treats they'd brought over. It was nice to just unwind, especially after the heavy conversation he'd had with Jamie. The guys were eager to hear more, so Ryan started recounting the strange chain of events that had led to Max becoming his dog.

Bandaid, who had been lounging with his paws behind his head, perked up at the mention of Jamie. "Wait, so you went back to see Jamie? What was that like? He's, like, super quiet and mysterious, right?" Seemingly uninterested in the whole story that Ryan had just laid out.

Ryan sighed. "Yeah, I went back to the daycare today. And Jamie—he's...he's hard to read. He's smart, really, like he put two and two together about Max in ways I hadn't even considered. But when I was there, I don't know...something about him just messes with my head. I feel like I'm totally out of my depth." He scratched his head nervously. "I mean, how could someone like Jamie even consider someone like me? Is he even gay? It's crazy, right?"

Lysander, who had been quietly sipping his drink, raised an eyebrow and looked at Ryan with a knowing look. "You're overthinking it, man. You've been doing that a lot lately." His tone was calm, but there was a sense of understanding in it. "Look, we all saw how he looked at you. The way he looked at you when you were talking about Max? You could tell he was into you. You were both practically fumbling over your words. It was obvious."

Bandaid laughed, nodding enthusiastically. "Yeah! Dude, it was like you two were both in your own little world. You couldn't stop looking at him, and he was all shy, glancing at you whenever you weren't looking. We saw the sparks flying from a mile away." He grinned, poking Ryan playfully. "You're just too scared to admit it."

Ryan groaned, rubbing his face in frustration. "It's not that easy, alright? I can't just—" He stopped himself, unsure of how to express it. "I don't know what to do with all of this. I've spent so long hiding who I really am. And now I'm starting to feel...attracted to Jamie? It just feels like I'm doing something wrong, like it's too soon to feel that way. I shouldn't be feeling this way so quickly."

Bandaid raised his eyebrows, giving Ryan a pointed look. "Weird? Dude, you've been hanging out with us, and we're all just doing our thing. You deserve to be with someone who cares about you, and it sounds like Jamie might be that person. You're being a little dumb, honestly. Like, all the signs are there, and you're still doubting it?"

Lysander leaned back, crossing his arms thoughtfully. "It's not about 'doing something wrong,' Ryan. You're allowed to feel how you feel. We all had to come to terms with who we are, and we've got your back. If you like Jamie, then that's a step in the right direction. The fear you're feeling—it's just holding you back. You know that, right?"

Ryan felt a knot in his stomach at the mention of his fear. The words of his friends were kind, but they were also a reminder of how difficult it still felt to embrace his true self. He'd spent years suppressing those feelings, and now they were surfacing with a vengeance. "But how do I even deal with this?" he murmured, looking down at his hands. "I've been hiding from who I really am for so long. It feels like all I've ever known is just to pretend, to live up to some ideal of what I should be. And now—"

"And now," Bandaid interrupted, his voice firm but gentle, "you get to be who you really are. It's that simple. You don't have to pretend anymore. And if Jamie's into you, then that's a pretty great reason to step out of your shell and start being real about it."

Lysander nodded, his face serious but encouraging. "You don't owe anyone an explanation. You don't have to rush anything, either. But if you feel something for Jamie, then that's something worth exploring. Just be honest with yourself, Ryan."

Ryan took a deep breath, his friends' words settling. "I know you're right. I've been fighting this for so long, trying to figure out the 'perfect' time to be real, but maybe it's not about finding the right time. Maybe it's about just taking the leap and seeing where it goes. I'm just scared of making a mistake... again."

Bandaid gave him a reassuring grin. "Look, we all screw up sometimes. But don't let that fear stop you from living your truth. Besides, you've got us in your corner, no matter what happens with Jamie." He leaned over to high-five Lysander. "And don't worry, we're all waiting for the day you finally admit that Jamie's been giving you *those* looks all along."

Lysander smirked, but his tone remained calm and supportive. "And when you're ready, you'll figure it out. Just don't let yourself be paralyzed by indecision. You deserve happiness, Ryan. Don't let it slip away."

Ryan smiled, feeling a warmth in his chest at the support his friends offered. Maybe it wouldn't be easy, but at least he wasn't alone in this anymore. He had to think of a way to see Jamie again.

The next day, Ryan walked into the daycare, feeling his heart race with every step. He spotted Jamie behind the counter, his usual calm and collected self, but something about today made Ryan feel jittery. His tail wagged nervously as he approached, his mind trying to focus, but Jamie's presence had that effect on him—stunning, magnetic, and hard to ignore.

Jamie glanced up as Ryan entered, his eyes immediately softening when he saw Max by Ryan's side. He gave Ryan a small, knowing smile, as if picking up on the bond they shared without a word being said.

"Hey, Ryan," Jamie greeted him, his voice warm but with a hint of playfulness. "I see Max is still sticking with you, huh?"

Ryan smiled nervously, his tail flicking behind him. "Yeah, he's, uh, mine now." He cleared his throat, trying to sound casual but failing miserably. "I decided to keep him. His original owner...passed away, and I couldn't just leave him." The words felt heavy, but he pushed through. "Max needed a home, and I guess I was there."

Jamie's expression softened further, his eyes filled with quiet understanding. "I'm really happy for you both. He's lucky to have you, Ryan."

"I'm the lucky one, honestly." He knelt down to pet Max, who leaned into the touch, his tail wagging furiously. "I wasn't sure what I was going to do at first, but now I can't imagine life without him."

Jamie chuckled, his ears flicking in amusement. "I get it. It's amazing how much love a dog can bring into your life." He looked at Max, his expression sincere. "You're doing a good thing, Ryan. You're giving him a second chance."

Ryan nodded, his throat tightening as emotion threatened to overwhelm him. "Yeah, I hope so."

Jamie smiled softly, and after a brief moment, he added, "I could make Max a proper tag if you want. Just to make it official."

Ryan blinked, a little surprised. "You'd do that?"

Jamie's smile widened. "Of course. It's the least I can do."

Ryan smiled back, his heart lightening just a little. "I'd really appreciate that."

They both moved to the counter, where Jamie began making the tag for Max. Ryan watched, still in awe of how naturally Jamie seemed to handle everything. As Jamie worked, Ryan's thoughts briefly drifted back to how much Jamie's presence affected him. It was hard to ignore how much he wanted to be close to this guy, to spend time with him.

When Jamie finished, he handed the tag over to Ryan with a smile. "Here you go," he said, his voice soft but genuine.

Ryan stood up, holding the tag carefully, his tail wagging a little as he clipped it onto Max's collar. As he did, he felt his eyes sting with emotion, and he quickly wiped a tear away from his cheek.

Jamie watched him, his expression softening even more. "I think it's really sweet how much you care for him," Jamie said, his voice low but sincere. "You're a good guy, Ryan. Plus, he looks so handsome with his new bling!" Jamie said, squishing Max's face in the derpiest way. "Handsome and goofy, like his owner," Jamie said, glancing at Ryan before patting Max's head once more.

Ryan's chest tightened, and he had to look away for a moment to compose himself. "Thanks, Jamie. I—uh—really appreciate you helping me out with this."

There was a brief pause as they stood there, and for a moment, Ryan almost convinced himself that this was just how things were supposed to be: him and Max, finding their way forward. But something in his heart pushed him to act, something deeper that had been building ever since he'd met Jamie.

He turned around, his heart pounding again. His tail flicked nervously behind him. *Just do it, Ryan,* he thought to himself. *Ask him out. Just do it.*

"Hey, Jamie?" Ryan called out, his voice wavering slightly as he turned back to face him.

Jamie raised an eyebrow, looking at Ryan curiously. "Yeah?"

Ryan swallowed hard, his ears folding a little in nervousness. "I was thinking...maybe you would want to grab coffee sometime?" He blurted the words out quickly, feeling his heart race faster than ever. "You know, if you're free..."

Jamie blinked, surprised, but a small smile began to tug at the corners of his mouth. His tail flicked behind him in a nervous gesture, and he took a moment before responding.

"I'd like that," Jamie said, his voice gentle but sincere. "Yeah, I'd really like that."

Ryan felt a surge of relief wash over him, though his tail wagged with both excitement and nervousness. "Great! I'll—uh—make sure work isn't screwing me over and making me work doubles again. I'll text you what day works best?"

Jamie nodded, his smile warm and inviting. "Sounds good."

As Ryan left the daycare, he felt lighter than he had in weeks. Max, wagging his tail happily at his side, looked up at him as they walked out together, and for the first time in a long time, Ryan felt like everything might finally be falling into place.

Chapter 6

RYAN stared at his phone for a moment, his thumb hovering over the keyboard. He'd typed out the message at least three times already, each version sounding either too eager or too formal. Taking a deep breath, he decided to keep it simple.

Ryan: *"Hey, Jamie. Would you be up for coffee this Saturday? There's a place just down the street from me I think you'd like."*

His heart thudded as he hit send, the whoosh of the message traveling through the ether making it feel suddenly real. He tossed the phone onto the couch as if it had burned him, running a hand through his hair with a nervous laugh.

Minutes passed—two? Five? It felt like an eternity before the soft ping of a notification pulled his attention. He scrambled to grab his phone, almost dropping it in his haste.

Jamie: *"That sounds perfect. What time?"*

Ryan exhaled, not realizing he'd been holding his breath. A smile crept across his face, small at first, then spreading wide enough to make his cheeks ache. His chest felt light, his heart thudding a little too fast, but in a way that reminded him of excitement rather than anxiety.

He texted back quickly, arranging a time and confirming

the details, but his focus wasn't entirely on the words. Instead, he found himself picturing Jamie's face—those moments when he seemed a little unsure, a little hesitant, but full of quiet determination. The thought made something in Ryan's chest shift, a kind of warmth he hadn't felt in a long time.

As he set his phone down, a strange mix of excitement and nervousness began to simmer. It wasn't just about the coffee; it was about seeing Jamie, getting to know him better. And maybe—just maybe—finding something they both needed.

Ryan leaned back, smiling to himself, his mind already spinning with possibilities. Coffee on Saturday felt like a small step, but one that could mean so much more.

Ryan hesitated before opening the group chat with Bandaid and Lysander. His tail flicked behind him, betraying the nervous energy he was trying to keep under wraps. After a few seconds of staring at the blank text box, he tapped out a message quickly before he could second-guess it.

Ryan: "Hey, just a heads-up, I've got coffee plans with Jamie this Saturday."

His ears swiveled forward in anticipation, listening to the faint vibrations of his phone as if it might help him predict their reactions. Sure enough, the chat exploded almost immediately, starting with Bandaid.

Bandaid: "*OH. MY. GOD. SHUT UP. Coffee plans?! Like, ACTUAL plans with Jamie?! I'm dying. This is so cute I could scream.*"

Ryan's tail thumped against the couch involuntarily as he read Bandaid's message. He knew the teasing was coming, but it still made the fur on the back of his neck bristle slightly. He started to type a reply, but Bandaid wasn't done.

Bandaid: "*Ryan, what are you even wearing? Wait, wait, don't tell me you're gonna show up in, like, your usual boring stuff. You need something that says, 'I'm hot, but I don't know it,' you know? Tail looking fluffy, ears on point. Ugh, you're gonna kill it.*"

Ryan snorted, shaking his head as his ears twitched. He hadn't even thought about his outfit yet.

Before he could reply, Lysander's message came through, slower but more deliberate.

Lysander: *"Bandaid, you're overwhelming him. Ryan, don't let him derail you with superficialities. What's important is your demeanor. Confidence, even if you don't feel it. Keep your ears relaxed, your posture open, and don't fidget with your tail. It sends the wrong message."*

Ryan blinked at his phone, his lips quirking up at Lysander's ever-serious tone. He could almost picture the regal way Lysander carried himself—always calm, tail curling with slow, measured movements that exuded control.

Ryan: *"Thanks, Lys. I'll try to keep my tail under control."*

Bandaid: *"LOL Lys, let him wag his tail! It's cute when he's happy. Jamie's gonna love it. Honestly, if I were Jamie, I'd swoon the second you walked in, Ryan. You're, like, unfairly adorable."*

Ryan's nose twitched, a faint heat spreading through his cheeks. He knew Bandaid was just being his bubbly self, but the way he said it made his chest feel strangely tight. His tail swished a little despite himself.

Ryan: *"Thanks, Bandaid. I'm just...nervous, you know? I don't want to overthink it."*

Lysander: *"Nerves are natural, but don't let them dominate you. Remember, Ryan, you're in control of this interaction. Engage with Jamie sincerely. Watch his ears and tail—his body language will tell you more than his words if you pay attention."*

Bandaid: *"OMG yes! If his tail wags even a little, you're in! Eee, I'm so excited for you. But you HAVE to text us after or I'll, like, explode. Literally."*

Ryan: *"You two are impossible."*

Bandaid: *"We're perfect, babe. You're welcome. You've got this!"*

Lysander: *"Indeed. And remember, no matter the outcome, this is progress."*

Ryan set his phone down, his ears twitching as he replayed their words. Bandaid's bubbly excitement made him smile, and Lysander's steady advice grounded him. His tail curled around his thigh, swishing once before settling. He could do this. Saturday wasn't just about coffee; it was about a step forward—and he wasn't doing it alone.

Ryan stood in front of his mirror, chewing anxiously on his lip as he ran a hand through his hair for what felt like the hundredth time. He had chosen a casual outfit that morning—slim-fit jeans cuffed at the ankles, a pair of edgy sneakers, and a simple, snug T-shirt that showed off the results of his time at the gym. He'd thrown on a flannel shirt, sleeves rolled up to reveal his forearms, giving the whole look a slightly hipster vibe. But despite all that, he couldn't get his hair to behave.

After another minute of fussing, Ryan let out a small groan and dropped his comb onto the dresser. "You know what, Max," he said, turning to his dog, "this is as good as it's gonna get. Don't judge me, okay?"

Max wagged his tail, ears perking in curiosity as Ryan bent down to give him a gentle scratch behind the ears. "Wish me luck, buddy," Ryan added, his voice quieter, almost conspiratorial. "Gotta go meet up with a cute boy...for a first date..." He stopped himself, shaking his head. "Just...wish me luck."

With one last glance in the mirror, Ryan grabbed his keys and headed out the door.

The café Ryan had chosen was a locally owned spot, tucked away on a lively street. From a distance, he spotted Jamie leaning against the brick wall outside, dressed in a soft-knit beanie that perched just so on his head. He wore a slouchy, oversized sweater that complemented the earthy tones of his brown-striped fur, paired with rolled-up chinos and a pair of worn-in sneakers. The overall look screamed low-key hipster, and Ryan couldn't help but smile to himself.

Jamie seemed a little awkward, his posture stiff, shifting from one foot to the other as if he didn't quite know where to put his hands. But the moment he saw Ryan approaching, his ears perked, and he stood up straighter, a small grin lighting up his face. Ryan's heart fluttered at the sight, and he found his own tail wagging softly, even though he tried to remain composed.

"Heh, you're always in such a good mood," Jamie commented softly, though his cheeks burned with a blush as he said it.

Ryan laughed, rubbing the back of his neck. "Yeah, well... some days, anyway. It's good to see you." He motioned toward the café's entrance. "Shall we head in?"

Jamie nodded, pulling the door open for Ryan. A rush of cool air washed over them, carrying the rich aroma of coffee beans, sweet syrups, and faint notes of spices. It made Ryan's nose twitch appreciatively, and as he inhaled, he caught the shy way Jamie glanced at him. The hyena's cheeks heated again, clearly finding Ryan's little sniff endearing.

Inside, the café was cozy but bustling with chatter. Exposed brick walls, scattered potted plants, and a chalkboard menu gave the place a down-to-earth charm. Oversized armchairs and small wooden tables were arranged in a way that balanced privacy with the lively hum of conversation. An inviting mix of indie music played in the background, blending seamlessly with the sounds of espresso machines and milk frothers whirring behind the counter.

Ryan led Jamie toward a small table in the corner, half-hidden by a tall shelf of coffee blends and mugs for sale. It felt private enough to talk without being entirely cut off from the café's gentle buzz. As they took their seats, a warm overhead light bathed them in a soft glow.

Ryan couldn't hide his excitement, and as he settled into his chair, he offered Jamie a wide smile. Across from him,

Jamie tugged at his sweater sleeves, his gaze flicking around uncertainly before returning to Ryan. Despite the flush in his cheeks, he managed a gentle grin.

"So," Ryan began, his tail wagging under the table, "I'm really glad you came. It's nice to, uh, hang out outside the daycare for once."

Jamie's ears flicked bashfully, and he nodded. "Yeah. Me too."

A moment of comfortable silence fell between them, punctuated only by the soft rustle of paper menus and the aromatic swirl of freshly brewed coffee in the air. Outside, life carried on in the bustle of the street, but in that quiet corner of the café, it felt like it was just the two of them, finally on the same page—if only for a morning cup of coffee together.

Ryan found himself talking far more than he'd expected to. Once he and Jamie had grabbed their drinks—a creamy latte for Ryan and a simple black coffee for Jamie—they settled back at the corner table, and Ryan began to share bits and pieces of his life. It started innocently enough, mentioning his shifts as a nurse, the ups and downs of his day-to-day, but before he knew it, the conversation snowballed.

He talked about his workouts at Bark Bell, how he was trying to push past a plateau on chest day, and how Bandaid and Lysander always teased him about being too serious at the gym. He even told a couple of stories about how Bandaid inevitably got everyone in trouble with his prankster antics, or how Lysander's matter-of-fact style set them all straight when things got too chaotic. Every now and then, he would pause to sip his latte, but the words kept flowing as soon as he put the mug down.

Jamie listened intently the entire time, his big, striped ears occasionally twitching as he nodded along. He gave small smiles, the corners of his eyes crinkling, or laughed lightly when Ryan hit a particularly funny moment in his story. From time to time, Jamie would lean in, resting an elbow on the table, his posture open and attentive. It was clear he was absorbed in everything Ryan was saying, even if he didn't interject much.

The background noise of the coffee shop faded into a gentle murmur as Ryan carried on, barely pausing except to take a breath or wet his throat. The more animated he became, the more he noticed Jamie's eyes following every gesture, soaking in each anecdote with quiet enthusiasm. Yet, eventually, Ryan realized how much time had passed. He glanced at his phone to check and nearly jumped—forty whole minutes had slipped by, and he'd barely let Jamie get a word in.

He halted abruptly, his tail giving a guilty little wag under the table. "Oh my God," he blurted, ears folding back in mortification. "I'm so sorry, I've been rambling on forever." He set his mug down carefully, cheeks warm with embarrassment. "I swear I didn't mean to talk your ear off."

Jamie blinked, then shook his head with a gentle laugh. "It's okay," he said softly. "I like listening to you. You're passionate about the people in your life...and your workouts, apparently." A faint flush tinted the insides of his ears, but his smile was genuine.

Still, Ryan couldn't help but feel a little self-conscious. He pressed his palms together on the table. "Yeah, but—" he shrugged, letting out a sheepish chuckle—"I want to hear about you, too. I just realized I've been hogging the floor here. Please, tell me more about...well, anything! I mean, I barely know what you do in your free time, or if you're still studying, or—" He let out another laugh, shaking his head. "I'm doing it again. Sorry, sorry. Let me just...hush and listen."

Jamie's shy smile grew a little wider. He sat up straighter, seeming appreciative that Ryan had noticed. "No, really, don't worry," he assured softly, voice carrying a gentle warmth. "I'm not used to talking this much about myself, but I'd love to share if you want to know."

Ryan nodded eagerly, leaning forward and resting his chin in his hand. "I definitely want to know," he said, lowering his voice as if it were a secret just for them. "Tell me everything."

Jamie hesitated for a second, his cheeks coloring, but there was a newfound spark in his eyes. He took a slow sip of his coffee, and then, with a small but determined breath, he began to speak.

Jamie began by confessing his love for computer video games, his voice quiet but tinged with enthusiasm as he explained how he'd always found digital worlds more compelling than sports fields. He admitted that in high school, he'd joined track and soccer teams mostly to please his parents—but it never really ignited his passion. "I mean, I like competing," he said, ears folding back slightly, "just…not in the way my folks wanted." He trailed off for a moment, his gaze dipping down, and Ryan sensed a flicker of hurt in Jamie's eyes—perhaps a deeper story of parental expectations. Yet Jamie caught himself, exhaling a quick breath before shifting topics.

"So, anyway…" he cleared his throat, brightening again. "I've been into this speedrunning game recently. It's like…you have to eliminate enemies as fast as possible, through a specific route in this jungle map." The tips of his ears twitched as he spoke, an excited spark lighting up his brown eyes. "I'm actually, uh…one of the top players in the country, I guess." His cheeks flushed at the admission, like he couldn't quite believe it himself. "I've never really said that out loud. Feels kind of geeky."

He started to ramble, suddenly ignited by his own passion. "But it's not just about being quick, you know? You have to memorize enemy spawn patterns and how they patrol certain areas of the map. There's one section, about three minutes into the run, where if you don't time your jumps perfectly over these fallen logs, you'll set off a trap and lose precious seconds. And then there's this hidden cave behind a waterfall—most new players miss it—but it's where you can pick up an ammo boost that basically ensures you can handle the rest of the level without reloading at the wrong time." Jamie paused, looking sheepish. "Sorry, I'm probably going into too much detail. I just...get really excited about it."

Ryan found himself leaning forward on the small table, captivated by Jamie's honest enthusiasm. His normally hesitant posture was relaxed, and he occasionally bared a glimpse of sharp, pearly-white canines whenever he laughed at himself. His eyes—deep brown with subtle flecks of gold—glowed with a quiet confidence as he outlined each strategic point.

Ryan realized he hadn't spoken in a while—he was too busy absorbing Jamie's every word, every flick of his ears, every curve of a grin that revealed just a little more of his personality. He stored mental notes: *He lifts his muzzle when he's excited; his voice quickens when he's really into something; he taps his foot under the table when he's proud but shy about it.*

Finally, Ryan cleared his throat. "That's...wow. That's impressive," he said, letting out a soft chuckle. "You're basically famous. I need your autograph," he teased, a playful glint in his eyes.

Jamie's blush deepened, and he ducked his head, a shy smile playing at his lips. "It's not a big deal," he murmured. "I just...really like it. It's something I feel good at."

Ryan let the warmth of Jamie's fervor sink in, silently marveling at how just a few minutes of listening to him opened a doorway into a deeper understanding of who this quiet, striped hyena really was—and how much more Ryan wanted to learn.

The conversation between Ryan and Jamie carried on for hours, the mellow hum of the coffee shop creating a soft backdrop for their easy chatter. Though Ryan rambled on about everything from funny nursing stories to the random chaos of daily life, Jamie never seemed bored. On the contrary, he leaned in, smiling and nodding at all the right moments, occasionally adding small anecdotes about games he liked or the music he'd been listening to. It was comfortable—*too* comfortable, perhaps, for two people who'd just begun to get to know one another.

Yet, despite the ease, both held back from talking about heavier topics. When Ryan's mind wandered to his past heartbreak or his rocky self-discovery, he changed the subject. When Jamie's eyes flickered with a hint of sadness, he'd steer the conversation elsewhere. It felt as though they both sensed the fragility of something new, something they didn't want to break just yet.

After what seemed like no time at all, Ryan glanced down at his phone and noticed the hour. He let out a small gasp. "Wow...it's getting really late." He scrolled through a couple of missed messages and realized with a pang of guilt that he needed to get home. "Max has been cooped up in my apartment for way longer than usual," he said, tail swishing anxiously behind him. "I should probably let him out...but, if you want to come with me—just to, y'know, hang out or...I dunno, meet Max again—"

Jamie froze for a split second, his eyes going wide. A flicker of unease crossed his face, and his ears folded back as he glanced at Ryan. Suddenly, he looked down at his own phone, clearing his throat. "Oh. Um..." he began, awkwardly shifting in his seat. "No thank you. I—I actually have to go too. It's getting late for me as well."

Ryan blinked, not understanding the shift in tone. "Oh—"

Jamie stood up quickly, nearly knocking his chair backward in his haste to leave. "Sorry," he mumbled, fumbling with his wallet and phone. His face was flushed, and he seemed unable to meet Ryan's gaze. "I should...get going. I'll...talk to you later. Thanks for the coffee."

Feeling panic twist in his chest, Ryan's ears flattened. He realized just how his invitation might have sounded. *Oh no, oh no. That's not what I meant at all.* He shot up from his seat and reached out as Jamie started for the door, his voice cracking with urgency. "Wait—Jamie, I didn't mean—! I wasn't—"

But it was too late. Jamie, ears pinned, was already out of the shop, the door's bell jangling in his wake. Ryan stood there, hand still half-extended, a sinking feeling knotting in his stomach as he watched Jamie disappear into the busy afternoon crowd. The sudden chill in the air told him something had gone very wrong, and he was left wondering how he could possibly fix it.

Ryan sat on the floor of his living room, leaning back against the couch with Max sprawled beside him. The golden-furred dog rested his head on Ryan's thigh, big brown eyes watching him intently as Ryan absently scratched behind Max's ears. A dull ache throbbed in Ryan's chest—he couldn't stop replaying Jamie's reaction in his head. *It totally sounded like a hook-up invitation,* he thought, cringing.

With a heavy sigh, he pulled out his phone and opened the group chat, where Bandaid and Lysander were still recovering from the play-by-play he'd given them after the coffee date fiasco.

Ryan: *Guys…I messed up. I was trying to be nice, but I basically asked Jamie back to my place in the most awkward way ever. I swear I only wanted to let Max out, but Jamie looked at me like I wanted him in my bed."*

Bandaid: *"WHY ARE YOU LIKE THIS?"*

Lysander: *"I'm going to translate that politely: You should have specified EXACTLY why you wanted him to come over."*

Ryan: *"I know. I'm an idiot. I just didn't think. I was worried about Max and also wanted to keep talking with Jamie…so I said something like, 'Hey, we can keep hanging at my apartment…'"*

Bandaid: *"DUDE. You gotta lead with 'I need to let the dog out, do you want to come meet him again?' Or something that's obviously not 'Netflix and chill.'*"

Ryan: "*I said something like, 'We can go back to my place if you want.' TOTALLY sounded like I wanted him in my bed. Ugh.*"

Max snorted as if in agreement, shifting his head onto Ryan's knee. Ryan patted the dog's face, murmuring, "I messed up, buddy."

Lysander: "*I think you can still fix it. Just text him and clarify. Apologize and explain you only meant to let Max out, no strings attached.*"

Bandaid: "*But not in a way that sounds like you REALLY want him. Because that might ALSO come off weird.*"

Ryan shook his head, heart pounding with embarrassment. He gave Max a gentle nudge, sighing. "They're right, though. I gotta fix it."

Ryan: "*I'll text him tomorrow. Let him cool off for a bit. Maybe explain it was just a misunderstanding.*"

Bandaid: "*Ryan, you are adorable. But you are also the dumbest, himbo-pilled, man alive sometimes.*"

Ryan: "*Thanks for the vote of confidence. [rolling eyes emoji] I'm gonna go bury my face in a pillow now.*"

Lysander: "*We love you, man. Don't beat yourself up. Stuff like this happens*".

Ryan couldn't help but smile at his phone, even as he felt the sting of the day's events. He tucked the phone away and ran a hand over Max's snout, rubbing gently.

"All right, you big goof," he mumbled to Max. "Time to figure out how not to scare off one of the cutest guys I've ever met."

Max just wagged his tail, nudging his nose under Ryan's arm for another pat, as if reassuring him that it would all be okay—eventually.

The next day at work, Ryan was perched at the nurses' station, his phone in hand as he typed and erased the same message to

Jamie for what felt like the hundredth time. His fellow nurses bustled around him—checking charts, conferring about patients, juggling the usual organized chaos—but he barely registered any of it. Every time his fingers hovered over "Send," doubt flooded him, and he'd hit backspace again.

One of his coworkers, a seasoned nurse named Teresa, noticed his exasperated expression and let out an exaggerated sigh. "Ryan, your face is about as twisted as those IV lines we cleared out this morning. What's going on?"

He glanced up, feeling heat creep into his cheeks. "I just... said something super awkward to this, uh, person I like," he said, tapping the phone's edge on the counter. "I invited him back to my place, but I swear, it was only to let my dog out. He thought I was trying to hook up."

Teresa's eyebrows shot up. "Ah, I see. Miscommunication 101." She leaned closer, crossing her arms. "So, what's your plan?"

Ryan shrugged, re-reading the half-finished text in his phone's draft. "I've been trying to word an apology—*or* a clarification, really—but nothing sounds right. I don't want to come on too strong, but I also don't want him to think I'm just brushing it off."

Teresa rolled her eyes playfully. "Ryan, you're a nurse. What do we do when we see something wrong with a patient's care or we're worried about a diagnosis?"

"We address it," he said, a faint smile tugging at his lips.

"Exactly. We're straightforward. We fix it. Why? Because in healthcare, withholding the truth is never a good idea." She tapped the desk meaningfully. "Look, if you liked spending time with him, just say so. Be honest. Maybe even share a bit of your history—why this is new and nerve-wracking for you. The truth beats tiptoeing around."

Ryan exhaled, feeling a swirl of relief and apprehension. "You really think I should just...put it all out there?"

Teresa nodded without hesitation. "Totally. If he's worth your time, he'll appreciate the honesty. And if not, well—at least you tried. But from what you've said, I think he will."

Ryan stared down at his phone once more, his heart thumping. Slowly, he began typing, letting Teresa's words guide him:

"Hey, Jamie. I'm sorry if I made you uncomfortable yesterday. I really did just need to let my dog out, and I'm still getting used to all of this—dating, being myself. I loved spending time with you. I hope you know it was purely an invite to hang out and meet Max again, not some weird come-on. You mean a lot to me already, and I'd never want to mess that up by being unclear."

His fingers hovered over the send button, and he glanced at Teresa, who gave him a thumbs-up. With a decisive tap, he hit "Send." Immediately, nerves flared in his chest, but there was also an odd sense of relief.

"That's more like it," Teresa said, snatching a couple of patient folders and pushing them into Ryan's hands. "Now, get back to work before I have to write you up for daydreaming on the clock, lover boy."

Ryan barked out a laugh, tucking his phone away. "Yes, ma'am," he replied, feeling a little lighter as he made his rounds—knowing that, for better or worse, he'd finally said what he needed to say.

Later that evening, Ryan was sprawled on his couch in gym shorts and a worn T-shirt, half-watching some reality show he'd clicked on just to fill the quiet. Max dozed at his feet, the occasional twitch of a paw the only sign the dog was dreaming. Amid the calm, Ryan's phone vibrated in his pocket, startling him out of his daze. Heart leaping into his throat, he fumbled awkwardly, nearly dropping the device as he hurried to fish it out.

His pulse pounded as he unlocked the screen and spotted Jamie's name at the top of his messages. The text loaded—a

GIF of a cat raising a suspicious eyebrow, underlined by the word *SUS*. Ryan's breath caught for an instant, but then a grin spread across his face. He let out a breathless laugh, immediately realizing that Jamie's playfulness was still intact. This wasn't a cold dismissal; it was teasing. His chest felt lighter, relief flooding him.

He stared at the GIF, replaying it a few times, his ears flicking with amusement. "Okay, so maybe he's not totally shutting me out," Ryan murmured, shifting to show Max the phone, as if the dog could understand. "See that, buddy? *Sus* is way better than silence."

Even though it was just a short reply, the quirky humor made Ryan's heart flutter. It was a sign—Jamie might still be open to talking, still curious. Gathering his courage, he hovered over his phone, debating how best to respond. He didn't want to come off desperate, but he also didn't want to miss the chance to keep the conversation rolling.

Finally, he typed a lighthearted reply, his mind buzzing with possibilities. Maybe, just maybe, he thought, there was still a chance to mend the misunderstanding and get to know the sweet, mysterious striped hyena on the other end of the line.

CHAPTER 7

RYAN glanced away from the TV to check his phone every few seconds, finding no new messages. He sighed, trying to focus on the program flashing on the screen, but his mind kept wandering. After sending a short, joking reply to Jamie's *SUS* GIF, he was expecting some immediate reaction—but there was nothing.

After a minute or so, he noticed the "typing" indicator pop up under Jamie's name. *Oh thank god,* he thought, his heart doing a little flip. He hunched over his phone, almost forgetting to breathe. The typing indicator flickered on...and stayed on... and *stayed* on.

Thirty seconds passed. A minute. *Is he writing a novel?* Ryan wondered, anxiety gnawing at his stomach. The signal would vanish, then reappear, then vanish again. Ryan felt Max shift by his side, the dog's tail thumping softly against the couch as if sensing Ryan's tension.

Eventually, the phone chimed with a new message, and Ryan scrambled to open it. His eyes zipped through the lines, his heart in his throat. But the response was surprisingly short:

Jamie: *"I'm sorry I just left like that. I have some stuff in my past that makes me panic. When things get stressful, I run. It's not your fault."*

Ryan read it three times, relief and worry mingling in his chest. Jamie had typed forever, but the final message was barely two sentences. *He must have been struggling with how to say it,* Ryan thought, a pang of empathy flaring.

Despite the brevity, Ryan could feel the weight behind Jamie's words. He could almost see the shy hyena, frowning at his screen, trying to condense years of complicated feelings into a single, vulnerable admission. *It's not my fault,* Ryan reminded himself, inhaling slowly. He started typing a reply, careful not to rush or pry too deeply, wanting only to reassure Jamie that he understood—and that he wasn't going anywhere.

Later that evening, Ryan sat cross-legged on his couch, phone in hand and Max curled up beside him. The living room lights were dim, casting a cozy glow across the room. His ears perked when his phone vibrated with a new message from Jamie, and he quickly unlocked it, tail wagging expectantly behind him.

He read Jamie's short but heartfelt explanation of how he tended to run when things got stressful. Ryan felt a pang of sympathy, recalling the look of panic on Jamie's face the other day. Leaning back into the cushions, he started typing with a warm smile:

"You're totally fine. Let's chalk it up to us being a little awkward with this whole thing. Listen, I was wondering if you're busy tonight? Maybe you'd wanna jump on Discord and show me some of your speedruns?"

His tail thumped a few times, betraying his excitement, and he absentmindedly scratched Max's ears while he waited for a reply. Eventually, his phone buzzed again. This time, the screen showed a GIF of a curious cat pushing a door open and peeking in. Right underneath, Jamie's message appeared:

"Yeah, that sounds really fun to me. But that means you'll have to see my Discord name, and I know you're going to make fun of me."

Ryan grinned, his ears wiggling in amusement. He typed

back quickly:

"*Mine's pretty bad too, so don't worry. I'll start: it's, uh...himbohyena69...*"

He sent the message and immediately clamped a hand over his muzzle, snickering at how ridiculous it looked in text. The phone buzzed again:

A GIF of a cat covering its mouth with its paws laughing hysterically popped into the chat.

"*That is so on brand for you, Mister Muscles.*"

Ryan chuckled, face feeling warm as he typed:

"*Oh yeah? And what's yours?*"

A notification suddenly popped up at the top of his screen: *You have added pawsniper to your friends list.* Ryan read it twice, his eyes widening. Then he let out a hearty laugh, tail wagging so hard that it thumped against the couch.

"*No freaking way.*"

Immediately, another message from Jamie appeared:

"*Shut up, shut up.*"

Ryan's grin was practically splitting his face at this point, and he typed with glee:

"*Well, I now know one of your kinks, and you shall be teased endlessly.*"

He followed that message with a picture—his phone camera capturing his large paws flexing back and forth in a mocking, playful way.

Jamie's reply was a single blushing emoji, followed by:

"*Wow, you really are evil.*"

Ryan, tail still wagging, shot back a tongue emoji, then:

"*Should I delete it? [wink emoji]*"

For a moment, the typing indicator flickered, then Jamie's response arrived:

"*...No.*"

Ryan couldn't hold back the burst of laughter that erupted from him. "You hear that, Max?" he said, rubbing the dog's ears. "I'm apparently evil." His grin was ear to ear as he tapped out a final message:

"Okay, I'll meet you on the computer!"

He jumped up, practically bounding to his desk, where he settled into his chair. Max flopped down on the rug nearby, tail lazily wagging. Ryan slipped on a pair of cat-eared headphones that glowed in a shifting rainbow of colors, the sight making him snicker at his own setup.

Once logged into his computer, he hopped into Discord, found *pawsniper*, and initiated a call. A pleasant ding rang through his headphones, and then he heard the soft rustle on the other end.

"Why *hello*, pawsniper," Ryan said, drawing out the greeting in a teasing tone.

There was a beat of silence before Jamie's exasperated sigh filtered through, accompanied by a quiet laugh. "Ugh...fuck you," Jamie muttered, though Ryan could hear the unmistakable smile in his voice.

Ryan's ears wiggled happily, and his tail gave a triumphant wag. This was a good sign: even if they were awkward, they were connecting, one joke at a time.

Ryan sat cross-legged at his desk, cat ear–shaped headphones perched comically atop his canine features. The irony of a canine wearing cat ears wasn't lost on him, and he couldn't help but smirk whenever he caught his reflection on the dark screen. Max, ever faithful, dozed at his feet, occasionally stirring when Ryan shifted or let out a sudden laugh.

He and Jamie were deep in a Discord call by then. Jamie had been guiding him through the ins and outs of a jungle-themed speedrunning game, pointing out every hidden shortcut and potential pitfall. Whenever the run demanded intense focus, Jamie's entire demeanor changed—his usually shy voice took on a serious edge, and Ryan, tail wagging behind him, hung on every word. Even the occasional cursing from Jamie, which made Ryan's ears flick in surprise, was a sign of his genuine passion rather than any anger at Ryan.

Over the course of a few hours, Ryan began to pick up tips here and there, and he even managed to spot an overlooked path at one point, causing Jamie to pause the game.

"Wait—are you telling me there's a whole route behind that waterfall?" Jamie exclaimed, ears twitching in disbelief.

Ryan chuckled, fiddling with the glowing cat ears on his headset. "Uh, yeah. The texture looked different, so I thought maybe there was something there."

To Ryan's delight, Jamie thanked him profusely and immediately restarted the section to incorporate this new shortcut, a determined grin audible in his voice. Despite the occasional stretches of silence—where Jamie needed to concentrate, or Ryan stared at the screen in fascination—Ryan never felt the awkward need to fill the space. He liked hearing Jamie's breathing, the clicks of his mouse, the hushed curses when a jump was mistimed.

It was only when Ryan stretched and noticed his apartment window had gone pitch-black outside that he glanced at the time. "Whoa," he said, ears perking straight up. "It's already two in the morning."

Jamie gave a soft sound of surprise on the other end. "Oh man...we've been at this for hours, huh?"

"Guess so," Ryan replied, stifling a yawn and accidentally bumping the mic on his cat ear headset. "Maybe we should call it a night."

There was a momentary lull as the ambient drumbeats of the paused jungle music echoed through their headphones. Ryan felt a comfortable warmth in that silence—like a gentle wave of contentment.

"I, uh, really loved this," he finally admitted, glancing at Max, who wagged his tail sleepily. "Hanging out with you like this...it was nice."

"I did too," Jamie said, clearly smiling on his end, though still with that shy undercurrent in his voice.

Ryan's tail gave a few more enthusiastic wags, and a playful grin lit up his muzzle. "Hey, Jamie?" he ventured, voice dipping to a more mischievous tone.

"Yeah?"

Ryan swallowed the flutter of nerves. "You're really pretty," he teased, letting out a breathy laugh. He could almost feel the sudden heat radiating from Jamie's cheeks through the call.

"S-stop," Jamie replied, half-laughing, half-muttering, though there was clear affection there. "You're pretty handsome yourself, you know."

They sat in that shared moment of mutual embarrassment and giddy happiness, unspoken words hovering between them. Eventually, Ryan cleared his throat. "I'll, um...text you tomorrow? Maybe we can do this again."

"I'd really like that," Jamie said softly. "Good night, Ryan."

Ryan grinned, removing the cat ear headphones and setting them on the desk. "Good night...*pawsniper*."

He heard a sputter of protest from Jamie followed by a bashful laugh before the call disconnected. With that, Ryan eased back in his chair and looked down at Max, who yawned wide and flopped onto his side.

"He thinks I'm handsome," Ryan said, ruffling the dog's fur. His heart felt light—he'd never had so much fun on a call before, nor felt so connected to someone in such a simple, honest way.

A soft ding from his phone broke his reverie. Picking it up, he found a GIF of an angry cat glaring. Below it, Jamie had texted: *"Imma hit you."*

Ryan couldn't stop the grin that spread across his muzzle. "He's *definitely* still shy," he remarked, letting out a warm laugh. "But hey, we're making progress."

He set his phone aside, flicked off the lamp at his desk,

and got ready for bed, excited for whatever tomorrow might bring—and for more teasing banter with the sweet, mysterious hyena who somehow made Ryan's late-night gaming sessions feel like the highlight of his day.

Ryan woke to the morning sun streaming through a gap in his curtains, the faint hum of traffic outside serving as his usual alarm clock. He rubbed the sleep from his eyes, rolled over, and reached for his phone. Most days, he'd scroll through his socials, check a few videos from the night before, and groggily warm up to reality.

But today was different. A notification blinked on his lock screen: Jamie had messaged him.

Ryan's tail gave an involuntary wag under the covers, a goofy grin forming on his muzzle as he tapped to read the text.

"Good morning. I hope you slept well."

Ryan's heart fluttered. He sat up, ears perking, and quickly typed out a response, half-smiling as he did.

"Mornin' to you too. Slept like a log. Did you dream about speedrunning?"

He watched the screen, noting the *typing*...indicator pop up. After a few seconds, Jamie replied:

"Ha, no speedrunning dreams...though that's not a bad idea. [laugh emoji]"

Ryan chuckled softly, flicking through his phone menu out of habit, almost hitting his usual social app before remembering Jamie was still chatting with him. *Way better than social media,* he thought, tail thumping beneath the sheets.

"Glad you got some rest. I found a hilarious video last night of someone trying to do a one-second world record for sneeze-canceling in your game. I'll send it to you—he was so sure it was a legitimate strat."

"Please do, that sounds amazing" Jamie responded.

They traded a couple more messages, each teasing the other

about silly internet finds from the previous night, until the conversation naturally meandered to their plans for the day.

"I'm basically just hitting the gym later. Gotta keep these muscles worthy of himbohyena69, right?"

Ryan cringed at his own playful brag, but he could practically feel Jamie's shy reaction.

"Haha, that's...so on brand for you. I'm just gonna look up some info on a new game that's dropping soon—platformer in space, sounds right up my alley."

Ryan's ears perked with interest as he fired back a response.

"Ooh, a cosmic jumping puzzle, huh? Sounds like I'd be tripping over everything."

A moment passed—Ryan could sense Jamie hesitating. Then another message came through, and his tail wagged in anticipation.

"Hey, uh...if you're free tonight, do you maybe want to go grab dinner? There's this pizza place I love. Best crust in the city."

Ryan felt his stomach flip, a smile creeping across his face that refused to leave. He let out a playful huff of breath, thumbs moving swiftly on the screen.

"Are you asking me on an official date, pawsniper? Because I'm so down for that.

He imagined Jamie's ears folding in bashful embarrassment on the other end and grinned.

"I—I mean, yes, if you want it to be a date..."

Ryan's tail wagged so hard it rustled the sheets.

"I accept your pizza-date proposal. My mouth's watering already—and not just for the food."

A couple seconds passed, then Jamie sent back a shy laughing emoji, followed by a simple,

"See you tonight, then?"

Ryan hopped out of bed, feeling lighter than ever.

"Absolutely. Time to get swole for our date. Talk soon!"

He set his phone on the bed, giving Max—who had poked

his head into the room—a quick pat on the head. "Pizza date, boy," Ryan murmured, trying to calm his racing heart. "Wish me luck."

Max wagged his tail, looking almost as excited as Ryan felt.

When Ryan arrived at the gym parking lot later in the day, he spotted Bandaid's car parked off to one side. The windows were cracked, the engine off, and he could just make out the silhouettes of Bandaid—the muscular white rabbit with trademark pink band-aids—and Lysander, the tall, refined purple werewolf.

Ryan slowed his steps, ears perking with curiosity. Inside the car, Bandaid and Lysander were leaning toward one another, exchanging flirtatious smiles. Bandaid giggled as he pressed a quick peck to Lysander's cheek, causing the werewolf's already rich purple fur to take on a deeper, embarrassed hue around his muzzle. Lysander let out a soft huff that was more flustered than disapproving, and he glanced away with a shy, matter-of-fact air.

That's when both of them noticed Ryan, who stood outside the driver's window, tail wagging in amusement.

"Oh—uh—hi, Ryan," Lysander said, trying to recover his composure. He cleared his throat, sliding out of the car with all the dignity he could muster. "I see you're...early today," he added, casting a quick glare at Ryan's knowing grin.

Ryan couldn't hold back his laughter as he leaned down, resting his arms on the roof of Bandaid's car. "Well, well," he teased, "don't let me interrupt your bunny-werewolf 'love fest'."

Bandaid stuck out his tongue, his fluffy tail wiggling in playful defiance. "Jealous, are we?" he shot back, winking as he hopped out of the car. He closed the door and sauntered around to Ryan, tapping a finger to one of his pink band-aids. "Besides, I thought you had a new boy toy to keep your mind busy?"

Lysander, still blushing under his fur, gave Ryan a very pointed, "Hmph," and straightened his posture. "I hardly think a simple peck on the cheek constitutes a 'love fest,'" he said, attempting to sound formal despite his ears folding back with embarrassment.

Ryan placed his hands on his hips, one brow arched. "Sure it doesn't. I didn't see *any* googly eyes or anything at all," he teased, stepping aside so the two could join him on the sidewalk.

Bandaid let out a mischievous giggle, skipping ahead to give Lysander a cheeky look. "Come on, Mr. 'Hardly Think,' we've got gains to make," he said, reaching out to gently pat the werewolf's arm.

Lysander tried to hold his stern expression, but his lips quirked into an involuntary smile.

Ryan trailed behind them, rolling his eyes good-naturedly. "You guys are too cute. Get a room already," he joked.

"Please," Lysander huffed, although his tail gave a small wag. "I'd prefer to maintain some level of dignity in public, unlike *certain* rabbits I know."

Bandaid shot him a playful smirk, his puffy tail wiggling at Ryan again. "Tsk, you're just mad I'm this cute," he retorted, then tossed over his shoulder at Ryan, "And as for you, I saw that grin. *Totally* envious."

They all broke into laughter as they entered the gym, stepping into the bustle of clanking weights and energetic music. In spite of the light roasting and teasing, Ryan felt an undercurrent of warmth—the comfort of real friends, each one open about who they were and unafraid to show a little affection.

A wave of warm, musky air hit them the moment they stepped onto the gym floor. The place was alive with the rhythmic clank of metal plates, the hiss of air pumps from exercise machines, and the sharp tang of sweat. Ryan inhaled, his part-hyena, part-golden retriever senses picking up on the heady scent—salt, iron, and the faint sting of disinfectant they used on the equipment. Bandaid and Lysander walked on either side of him, each one sporting the sheen of a budding workout: Bandaid's stocky rabbit form showed off his defined shoulders, pink band-aids seemingly stuck at random places on his arms and legs, while Lysander's tall, purple-furred physique made him stand out among the crowd.

They clustered near the free-weight section, where Bandaid wiggled his nose in curiosity, turning to Ryan with a grin. "So," he began, eyes bright with mischief, "did I hear something about you apologizing to your new boyfriend last night?" He waggled his eyebrows, leaning in. Lysander let out a soft groan, half amused, half exasperated, but Ryan just rolled his eyes and chuckled.

"Look," Ryan said, grabbing a couple of dumbbells and shifting them in his hands, "I sent Jamie a text explaining the whole 'invite to my place' disaster. He responded, we cleared it up, and then...we ended up on Discord. We spent hours on voice chat—he showed me some of his speedrunning stuff. It was actually awesome." He paused, ears flicking happily. "We lost track of time, almost until two in the morning."

Bandaid's ears perked, that grin never leaving his face. "Oh yeah? Speedrunning, eh?" he asked, giving Ryan's bicep a poke. "Is that what the kids are calling it now?"

Lysander shot him a pointed look, arms folded across his broad chest. "Stop," he said flatly, though a hint of a smile lingered at the corner of his muzzle. "Ryan, ignore this rabbit's innuendo."

"Believe me, I'm used to it," Ryan said with a laugh. He took a seat on a nearby bench, setting his weights down. "It was purely gaming, but we talked a lot, too. He's sweet, but I only know bits and pieces about him. Like, he's into speedrunning, he loves this weird coffee brand from some niche roaster, but...that's about it." He hesitated, thinking about Jamie's shy demeanour. "I realized I don't even know his favorite color or his biggest pet peeves. Maybe I should start asking more basic questions?"

Bandaid, mid-stretch, twisted to face Ryan. "So you don't even know if he's into candlelit dinners or scenic hikes?" The rabbit's big eyes glimmered as though these were life-or-death questions.

"Bandaid," Lysander warned, though softer this time. "Let him figure things out at his own pace."

Ryan shrugged, half-smiling. "He just invited me to dinner tonight, so I guess we'll see. I'm sure more will come out naturally over pizza." He picked up the weights again, standing to do a set of curls. "But yeah...you guys have any other suggestions on what I should ask or talk about? I don't want it to feel like an interrogation."

Bandaid's tail flicked behind him mischievously as he grabbed a barbell. "Well, you *could* ask what—"

"Let's keep it PG, please," Lysander cut him off, pressing his palm gently over Bandaid's muzzle.

Ryan laughed, finishing his first rep. Even amid the clang of equipment and the swirl of sweaty air, he felt a sense of warmth and contentment. He might not know everything about Jamie yet, but with friends like these, he was sure he'd figure things out—and have plenty of good stories to tell in the process.

Bandaid set his barbell down with a soft clang, ears perking up as he turned to Ryan, a mischievous glimmer in his eyes. "Okay, serious question," he said, dusting off his paws. "What *really* catches your eye when you look at Jamie? Like, how'd he get you hooked so fast?"

Ryan paused, taking a moment to adjust the weights on his dumbbells. A shy grin flickered across his face, and his tail gave a hesitant wag, betraying how much he enjoyed talking about Jamie. "Wow, where do I start..." He exhaled, leaning against the bench. "He's just...quiet, but in a way that makes you lean in, you know? It's like he's careful with his words, but once you get him talking about something he loves—like speedrunning—his whole face lights up. His eyes, man...they're this deep brown, kind of speckled with gold if you look close enough. I swear they sparkle when he's excited."

As he spoke, Ryan's eyes grew distant, recalling Jamie's shy smile. "And he does this cute thing when he's nervous—his ears fold back just a bit, but not all the way. Like he's *this* close to shutting down, but then he recovers, and it's so vulnerable, it just...I don't know, it makes me want to protect him and cheer him on. He's got that striped fur, right? But it's really soft-looking, especially around his cheeks. You can see it puff out a bit when he laughs. And then, oh!—" Ryan let out a small laugh, remembering another detail. "—Sometimes he bites his lower lip when he's concentrating. I noticed it while he was playing that game last night. It's this tiny thing, but it's...I don't know. It's real."

Bandaid's cheeks took on a subtle pink hue beneath his fluffy white fur. He hopped off his bench, fiddling with one of his ever-present band-aids. "Aww, man," he said, voice lilting with teasing affection. "That's, like, *really* sweet. You're all starry-eyed."

Lysander, who had been quietly listening from the side, gave a small, contented smile, his ears angled in approval. "It certainly sounds like you've been struck by the proverbial love bug," he mused, voice laced with his usual careful politeness. "It's nice to hear you speak so fondly of someone...I can't recall you ever being this earnest."

Ryan scratched the back of his neck, his own cheeks warming. "Guess I never really let myself feel like this before," he admitted softly. "It's weird, but good-weird, you know? I mean, I'm still nervous as hell."

Bandaid snickered, fluttering his lashes with exaggerated drama. "Awww, Ryan's in loooove." His fluffy tail wagged behind him, and he teased in a sing-songy voice, "*Somebody's got it baaaad.*"

Lysander rolled his eyes, though the grin on his muzzle gave him away. "Let him have his moment without your theatrics, rabbit."

Ryan joined in their laughter, shoulders relaxing as he realized just how much better it felt to open up. For the first time in ages, he felt something bright and genuine blossoming in his chest.

After a grueling workout—weights racked, mats tidied, and hearts still pounding—the trio made their way to the locker room. The clang of iron and the buzz of gym chatter faded behind them, replaced by the echo of running water and low murmurs from others freshening up. A warm, steamy haze hovered in the tiled space, intensifying the scent of shampoo, body wash, and damp fur.

Ryan tugged off his sweat-soaked shirt, golden-hyena fur matted down in places from the intensity of the session. His broad shoulders and toned arms still carried the post-pump burn, and he rolled his neck, relishing the small pops of relief. Lysander, towering and leanly muscled in that unmistakably graceful werewolf way, tossed his towel over a hook. A faint blush crept into his cheeks—evident even under purple fur—though he kept his composure, ever the picture of polite reserve.

Bandaid, meanwhile, waddled in with his own brand of swagger, peeling off a snug workout shirt that seemed to cling to every inch of his stout, muscular frame. His white fur, now damp with sweat, was plastered close to powerful arms, and the trademark pink band-aids sat askew on his biceps and thighs. But the real showstopper was how disproportionately large his thighs and backside were—quads bulging, glutes shaped like a bodybuilder's dream. Ryan couldn't help a playful smirk; he and Lysander had joked more than once that Bandaid might out-lunge them all combined.

Steam rose as they stepped into the communal showers, water cascading over fur and sending rivulets down well-defined chests and abs. Ryan scrubbed at his arms, letting out a content sigh as the hot water eased the tension in his muscles. Lysander stood a short distance away, face tilted up so that the shower spray drenched his muzzle, droplets streaming along firm shoulders and down lean flanks. His ears flicked, releasing stray droplets that splashed against the tiles.

Bandaid took the showerhead at the far end, fiddling with the temperature before stepping under the stream. His thick thighs flexed beneath the water, water droplets rolling along the curve of his muscular legs. He let out a satisfied hum, turning to keep a watchful eye on one of his band-aids that threatened to peel off in the steam.

"Need any help keeping that from falling off?" Ryan teased over the rush of water, raising his voice to be heard.

Bandaid stuck out his tongue in response, swirling around to rinse the suds from his fur. "Don't get too used to seeing *all* my best angles," he said with a hearty laugh, though his puffy tail wiggled smugly.

Lysander, cheeks still a faint red, cleared his throat in that formal way of his. "I think we've seen more than enough angles for one day," he remarked dryly, wiping water from his brow.

Ryan let out a chuckle, and for a moment, the three of them just enjoyed the soothing warmth of the showers—friends who'd worked hard, teased harder, but always had each other's backs. It wasn't merely about rinsing off sweat; it was a ritual of camaraderie, banter echoing under the steady hiss of running water, each one content to stand shoulder to shoulder with absolutely nothing to hide.

When Ryan finally got home from the gym, the sun was already starting its late-afternoon descent, painting the living room in a golden glow. Max trotted up eagerly to greet him, tail swishing in lazy arcs. Ryan gave his loyal companion a few well-deserved ear scratches, then bounded into his bedroom, mind abuzz with excitement for his dinner plans.

He flicked on the light and surveyed his closet like a hunter stalking prey. The first attempt was a pair of skinny jeans and a fitted T-shirt—too tight, he decided. *Need something more casual, more me.* He tugged off the shirt, tossing it onto a growing pile of rejections. Next, he tried a loose jogger style with a sleeveless hoodie. A glance in the mirror, a swift shake of his head—no, he looked like he was heading to the gym again.

He huffed, tail flicking in mounting impatience, then launched into a full-blown outfit marathon. Baggy trousers were next—draping comfortably over his hips, with just enough extra room around his thighs to give that effortlessly chill vibe. Nodding in approval, he added an oversized tee that hung just right against his half-hyena, half-golden retriever frame. But it wasn't quite complete.

Leaning toward the mirror, he experimented with chains—silver first, then a chunkier gold one. He pursed his lips, tilting his head, imagining what Jamie would think. Gold won out, catching a touch of the waning sunlight and gleaming warmly against his fur. A grin spread across his muzzle as he placed it around his neck, ears twitching in satisfaction.

Still not done, he rummaged through his shoe rack until he found his high-top sneakers—white with a few bold color accents that popped. He slid them on, lacing up swiftly, then stood in front of the mirror for the grand reveal: baggy pants, oversized shirt, gold chain, high tops. It looked...put together, but in that effortlessly cool way he'd been aiming for.

He tried out a few goofy poses, tail wagging behind him, then practiced a few smoldering looks in the reflection—failing hilariously, given the giddy grin that kept overtaking his face. "C'mon, focus," he muttered, stifling a laugh as he puffed his cheeks and tried again. Max peeked his head in from the hallway, ears pricked in curiosity at his owner's antics.

Finally, Ryan exhaled, letting go of the tension in his shoulders. "This'll do," he proclaimed, smoothing a paw across the oversized shirt. The outfit felt right. Confident but comfortable—just the right balance for a night with Jamie. He scooped up his keys, gave Max a gentle scratch on the head, and headed out the door, heart thudding with anticipation.

Chapter 8

Ryan slipped into the pizza parlor's lively atmosphere, the air heavy with the aroma of garlic, melting cheese, and freshly baked dough. The neon sign outside had hinted at a casual, comforting vibe, but inside, the buzz of conversation and the gentle hum of a jukebox in the corner made everything feel extra warm. He spotted Jamie seated at a small, rustic table near the back, his striped hyena ears twitching in time with the chatter around him. Jamie was hunched over a basket of breadsticks, absently picking at them and scanning the room—until Ryan decided to make a little playful entrance.

Quietly, Ryan crept up behind Jamie, trying not to laugh at how consumed he looked by the swirl of the restaurant. In one quick motion, Ryan covered Jamie's eyes with his hands. "Guess who?"

Jamie let out a startled chuckle, his ears perking. Almost instantly, his paws flew up to meet Ryan's. "Ryan," he said, half-laughing. He held onto Ryan's hands a second longer than necessary, the warmth of his touch sending a flicker of heat up Ryan's arms. "You dork," Jamie added with a broad smile, releasing Ryan's fingers to look up over his shoulder.

Ryan felt a sudden rush of blood to his cheeks as he slipped around to take the seat across from Jamie. His tail gave a telltale wag beneath the table, though he hoped it wasn't too obvious. "What can I say—I like to make an entrance," he teased, before nodding at the breadbasket. "Couldn't wait for me, huh?"

Jamie flushed lightly. "I was starving," he admitted, pushing the basket toward Ryan. "Here. You can have the rest. I didn't realize I was so hungry until I started nibbling on these."

"Don't mind if I do." Ryan grabbed a piece and took a hearty bite. His eyes drifted to the menu, but Jamie spoke up first.

"So, my favorite pizza here is a simple one: fresh mozzarella, basil, tomatoes...Kinda like a Margherita, but they do something with the sauce that makes it tangy. I can't get enough of it," Jamie said, ears flicking a bit as he gushed.

Ryan's eyes lit up, a grin splitting his muzzle. "Then that's what we get," he said, no hesitation in his voice. "Lead the way, oh wise pizza connoisseur."

Jamie laughed softly, motioning for the server. They placed their order—a large Margherita plus half a side of garlic knots—because, as Ryan insisted, "You can never have too many carbs." Once the server left, they settled more comfortably at the table.

While they waited, Ryan found himself picking at the remaining bread in the basket. He started recounting bits of his week at the hospital—some lighthearted moments with coworkers, a not-so-funny fiasco with a cart of medical supplies toppling over, and how the busyness of it all felt off.

"Work's okay," he said with a shrug, "but it's not the same anymore."

Jamie tilted his head, ears angled to show curiosity. "Not the same how?"

Ryan pressed his lips together for a moment, a pensive look in his eyes. "There was, uh...someone I used to be really close with there—Sam. I..." He hesitated, not wanting to reveal *too* much about Chloe or his coming out just yet. "Sam was important to me. We tried, but it didn't work out. Now, the place feels...a bit empty without him, I guess."

Across the table, Jamie's ears went from a curious tilt to something more subdued. He fiddled with the edge of a napkin, not entirely sure how to respond. "Oh," he said softly. "I'm sorry. That must be tough."

Ryan realized instantly that maybe he'd overshared, dropping a piece of emotional baggage that Jamie might not have been ready for. He opened his mouth to apologize, feeling that wave of guilt surface, but before he could, Jamie took in a slow breath and spoke up, his eyes darting to the table as though he couldn't quite meet Ryan's gaze.

"I, um..." Jamie began, voice wavering. "I had an ex, too. It was..." He swallowed, absently tapping a claw on the tabletop. "It was emotionally abusive, if I'm honest. And manipulative."

Ryan immediately sobered, giving Jamie his undivided attention. "That sounds awful," he said gently, leaning forward. "You don't have to—"

But Jamie continued, voice trembling. "He seemed so nice at first, y'know? But then it got...controlling. I'd do something I enjoyed—like gaming or going out with friends—and he'd act like I was abandoning him. He made me feel like I had to be responsible for his happiness. That if I didn't, I was being selfish or...or a bad boyfriend."

Ryan could see tears welling in Jamie's eyes, and his own chest tightened with sympathy. "Jamie..." he said quietly, but the hyena pressed on.

"He'd guilt-trip me over small things, like not texting back immediately or skipping a weekend trip to be in a tournament. I started giving everything up. I didn't want him to be upset, but it still never felt enough." Jamie's voice cracked, and he looked away, tears threatening to fall.

Ryan reached across the table and gently placed his paw over Jamie's, ignoring the swirl of onlookers enjoying their dinners. Jamie's cheeks burned under his fur as he glanced down at their joined hands, a single tear escaping down his stripe-marked muzzle.

"I'm sorry," Jamie muttered, trying to pull his paw back. "I shouldn't—this is supposed to be a fun dinner. I don't want to ruin it by dumping my problems."

Ryan gave his paw a reassuring squeeze, refusing to let go. "Don't apologize," he said, his own ears tilted forward in earnest concern. "I asked. I want to know these things, if you're comfortable sharing. And you have nothing to be sorry for."

Jamie sniffed, wiping at his eye with his free hand. For a moment, the tension hung between them, thick as the cheese that was probably on its way to their table. Then, with a shaky exhale, Jamie offered a tiny, grateful smile.

"Thanks," he whispered. "I don't...talk about that often. It's just, I guess hearing you mention Sam made me realize I've never really explained to anyone why I panic sometimes...or why I run."

Ryan nodded, giving Jamie's hand one more gentle squeeze before letting go. "Anytime you want to talk, I'm here," he said softly. "Really."

Just then, the waiter arrived with their pizza, and Ryan withdrew his hand, though the warmth of Jamie's touch lingered on his fur. As the waiter slid the steaming pizza onto the table, neither Ryan nor Jamie acknowledged the server beyond a polite murmur of thanks. They were still locked in a moment of mutual understanding, each of them trying to digest the heavy confessions that had just passed between them.

As they dug in, the conversation shifted to lighter things—favorite toppings, bizarre pizza experiments, and the comedic horrors of cheap frozen meals. But an unspoken bond now hovered between them. They'd each revealed a piece of a past that still weighed on their hearts, and though the stories were incomplete, it felt like a significant step.

They kept talking—Ryan occasionally wiping sauce off his muzzle, Jamie offering a half-smile whenever their eyes met. And when the final piece was devoured, they both leaned back, satisfied, each with a secret sense of relief that the other hadn't run away. On the contrary, they were still there, sharing space, vulnerability, and a promise of more tomorrows, however tentative they might be.

Ryan glanced across the table, a dazzling grin stretching across his muzzle as he admired the boy—no, *man*—sitting there in the soft glow of the restaurant's overhead lights. Something inside him stirred, a wild, exhilarating feeling that made his heartbeat thunder in his ears. He settled the bill before Jamie could even peek at it, provoking a playful growl of protest from Jamie, who then let out a resigned laugh.

As dinner drew to an end Ryan skillfully lunged for the bill before Jamie could even protest and placed his card inside. Ryan blushed and grinned proudly, "I will pay for dinner if you take a stroll with a smelly dog after this?"

"Thank you," Jamie rolled his eyes, standing up. "A walk sounds great."

Together they stepped out into the evening air. The sun was hovering at the horizon, drenching the city in swaths of orange and pink. They strolled side by side, eventually winding up at a small neighborhood park. Under the gilded light, Ryan couldn't help noticing how the sunset painted itself across Jamie's stripes and lent his eyes a burnished glow. Feeling a sudden flush, Ryan dropped his gaze to his sneakers, trying to regain composure.

"I know you have a complicated ex story," Ryan said quietly, stuffing his hands into his pockets. "I...I do too. Mine involves, uh, religion. I was raised in this strict environment, and I ended up hurting someone—a girlfriend named Chloe—by not being honest about who I was. I guess I was kind of...emotionally abused too. Or maybe just manipulated. It's messy, but basically I learned to hide. And then one day I realized..." He trailed off, exhaling through his nose. "I never stopped hiding."

Jamie listened intently, nodding in understanding, ears flicking back in empathy. Once Ryan finished, Jamie gently reached for his paw and laced their fingers together, a warm and silent show of support. Ryan's heart fluttered at the contact. "Seems like we both have some hard stuff to carry," Jamie said softly, squeezing Ryan's paw with a blush dusting his cheeks. Ryan squeezed back, marveling at how easy it felt to open up with him.

They wandered for a while longer, the city lights gradually taking over as dusk settled into true night. Eventually, they circled back to the spot where they'd started. Now the streetlamps gave everything a soft, silver glow, casting elongated shadows on the sidewalk. Ryan paused beneath one of those lamps, turning to Jamie with a tender smile and gently taking hold of both his paws.

"You are..." Ryan began, pausing as though searching for the right words. His tail wagged slowly behind him, betraying his nerves. "You are something so unique and special," he finished, his voice low but certain.

Jamie's ears flattened shyly, and a deep crimson warmth lit his muzzle. "Oh, stop." He chuckled, eyes flicking downward. "I'm nothing special at all."

Ryan drew in a breath, heart pounding. "I think you are," he insisted, voice cracking just a bit. Their eyes met, and he found himself drawn to the shape of Jamie's lips—the soft curve, the faint shine, how they quivered slightly as Jamie tried to steady his breath. He moved closer, and Jamie mirrored him, a quiet acceptance passing between them.

Then, gently, they leaned in, lips meeting in a tentative, shared warmth. In that moment, the world seemed to hush around them—traffic noise dulled, the night breeze paused, and all that existed was the press of lips, the racing of hearts. It was a slow, deliberate kiss that built into a moment of passion neither had anticipated. Ryan's paws slipped around Jamie's waist, pulling him close, and he felt Jamie tense for a fleeting second before melting into the embrace. Jamie let out a tiny, vulnerable whimper, his hands settling on Ryan's shoulders as he responded, breath hitching when Ryan's muzzle brushed more firmly against his own.

An intense bloom of emotion flared in Ryan's chest, unlike anything he'd felt before—a heady mixture of relief, desire, and a sweet sense of rightness. Their tails wagged behind them, inadvertently bumping together. The kiss lingered, slow and exploratory, until they finally broke apart, both of them gasping softly, foreheads nearly touching.

"That was...wow," Ryan managed, the tip of his tongue darting across his lower lip as though still tasting the moment.

Jamie released a soft, embarrassed laugh, his cheeks aflame. He couldn't seem to speak—could only nod and let out a slightly shaky exhale. The night air felt charged, crackling with the promise of something brand new and alive between them. And for the first time in a long while, both of them dared to believe that maybe, just maybe, they had found a piece of happiness worth holding onto.

The warmth of their kiss still lingered as they slowly stepped out of their little bubble under the streetlight. The night air felt crisp against Ryan's heated face, his heart still hammering in his chest as they walked toward Jamie's car. Their fingers brushed briefly before Jamie pulled his paw away, shoving it into his hoodie pocket in that shy way Ryan was already starting to recognize. The striped hyena still looked a little dazed, his tail flicking absently behind him as they strolled in silence for a few moments, both soaking in the energy of what had just happened.

As they reached Jamie's car, Ryan hesitated for a second, unsure how to extend the moment just a little longer. Then, a thought popped into his head. "Hey," he said, rubbing the back of his neck, golden fur ruffling under his touch. "You got a *Barkstergram?*"

Jamie blinked up at him, ears twitching slightly. "Oh, uh... yeah, I do," he said, pulling out his phone. "I don't post much, though."

Ryan grinned, tilting his head. "That just means I get to learn all the mysterious Jamie facts through careful stalking." He wagged his tail playfully.

Jamie let out a small, embarrassed chuckle but handed his phone over, letting Ryan type in his handle before following Ryan back on his own account. Their fingers brushed again as Ryan returned the phone, and for a second, neither of them moved. Ryan could still feel the pleasant buzz of their kiss thrumming beneath his skin, and acting purely on instinct, he leaned in and placed a small, lingering kiss on Jamie's cheek.

Jamie stiffened for a fraction of a second before melting under the touch, his ears flattening against his head as his face bloomed with color. "You're ridiculous," he muttered, though his tail gave him away, swishing happily behind him.

Ryan laughed and stepped back, shoving his hands into his pockets. "Drive safe, pawsniper," he teased.

Jamie groaned, rubbing his face, but when he looked up, there was that soft, glowing smile again. "You're never gonna let that go, huh?"

"Absolutely not." Ryan grinned and took a step back, waving as Jamie opened his car door. "Goodnight, Jamie."

Jamie settled into his seat, pausing for just a moment before softly replying, "Goodnight, Ryan." With one last lingering glance, he shut the door, started the engine, and drove off into the quiet city night.

Ryan stood there for a few seconds, watching the red glow of Jamie's taillights disappear down the road. His tail flicked lazily behind him as he exhaled a deep breath, feeling light, almost giddy. It had been *so long* since a date had left him feeling this way. Not just excited—but warm, like something real was beginning to take shape.

When he got home, Max greeted him at the door with an excited bark, wagging his whole body as Ryan knelt down to ruffle his ears. "Guess what, buddy?" he murmured, still grinning. "We might really like this one."

After kicking off his sneakers, Ryan flopped onto the couch, pulling out his phone. His notifications were already pinging with Jamie's follow request and a message that simply read:

"Made it home. Thanks for tonight."

Ryan's heart gave a stupidly strong thump in his chest, and he bit back a smile as he sent back:

"Anytime. Sleep well, cute stuff."

Shaking his head at himself, he tapped over to Jamie's profile. Just as Jamie had warned, his page wasn't flooded with posts—just a handful of carefully chosen moments. Ryan scrolled through them with curiosity, ears flicking forward as he pieced together little fragments of Jamie's life.

There were photos of vinyl records stacked on a shelf, one with a caption about *never trusting someone who doesn't love a good album from start to finish.* Ryan chuckled, realizing Jamie was into alt-rock and indie music—just like he was. Another post showed a dark-lit arcade, with a blurry image of a high-score screen and a joking caption about *wasting hours of my life for this one moment of glory.*

Ryan smiled as he kept scrolling, enjoying the way these tiny glimpses into Jamie's world made him feel like he was learning him in a whole new way. But then—his thumb stopped on a tagged post.

Happy 21st to this quiet but brilliant little menace. Hope this year is full of high scores and no tech malfunctions.

Ryan blinked. *21st birthday?* His heart did a small, awkward flip as he quickly scrolled back up to Jamie's profile. His mind did the math in a heartbeat. *Jamie is 21. I'm...27.*

A small wave of anxiety crept up his spine. It wasn't like six years was an enormous gap, but it was *enough* to make Ryan pause. Jamie was still so *young.* Just starting to really figure out adulthood. Ryan, on the other hand, had gone through a long, complicated past, years of denial, a painful breakup, and only now was he truly stepping into himself.

Was this...bad? Was it weird?

He exhaled, rubbing his forehead. He *liked* Jamie—a lot. That much was obvious. But what if Jamie wasn't looking for something serious? What if, in a year or two, Jamie realized he wanted something different? Someone younger, closer to where he was in life?

Ryan swallowed down the small knot in his throat. He hadn't even *talked* to Jamie about what either of them wanted yet—was he really going to start spiraling over a number?

Max let out a soft huff, sensing Ryan's shift in mood, and nudged his head against Ryan's side. Ryan blinked, then sighed, scratching behind Max's ears. "I'm overthinking, huh?"

The dog just wagged his tail, oblivious but comforting nonetheless.

Ryan sighed again, closing his phone for now. He'd talk to Jamie about it—when the time was right. For now, he'd let himself enjoy the glow of the evening, the lingering feeling of Jamie's lips against his, and the fact that, for the first time in a long time, he *wanted* to see where something led.

Ryan stared at his phone for a while, thumb hovering over the screen as he chewed on his lip. The feeling of Jamie's lips, the way his eyes had softened just before they kissed, the warmth of his paw in Ryan's—it all replayed over and over in his mind like a song he couldn't shake. He liked this boy. He really liked this boy.

But that nagging thought—the six-year gap—itched in the back of his brain, refusing to let him just be happy for one damn night. He needed to talk to someone who wouldn't just tease him endlessly (Bandaid was out of the question), someone who would actually listen and give solid advice.

He scrolled through his contacts and tapped on Lysander.

"Hey, you up?"

The reply came almost immediately.

"Of course. Is something wrong?"

Ryan exhaled through his nose. Typical Lysander—formal, composed, and always perceptive. He shifted against the couch, scratching Max's head absentmindedly as he typed.

'I don't know if "wrong' is the word, but I need your input on something. It's about Jamie."

"I assumed as much. Go on." Lysander replied.

Ryan hesitated for a moment, trying to find the right words.

"So, we had dinner. It was really good. We talked a lot—like, a lot. I told him some stuff about my past, and he told me some things about his. And then...we went for a walk, and we kissed."

There was a longer pause before Lysander's response popped up.

"I see. And how do you feel about it?"

Ryan sighed, rubbing his forehead.

"Like my brain is short-circuiting. I mean, the kiss was amazing. And I really like him. He makes me feel different than I ever have before. Excited, but also...comfortable? Safe? I don't know, man. I just know I want to be around him."

Another pause.

"That all sounds rather promising. So, what is it that's bothering you?"

Ryan sucked in a breath. *Here goes.*

"I found out he's 21."

There was an even *longer* pause this time. Ryan could practically see Lysander's furrowed brows as he processed the information.

"And you're 27."

"Bingo," replied Ryan.

Lysander took a minute to reply again, and Ryan started bouncing his leg, tail flicking anxiously against the couch cushion.

"Is it just the number that concerns you, or are you afraid of what that number means?"

Ryan groaned, letting his head flop back. Trust Lysander to get straight to the real question.

"I don't know, man. I guess I just worry that we're in totally different places in life. I've been through so much—figuring out my sexuality, dealing with Chloe, all the religious stuff. Jamie's just starting his 20s. What if he changes his mind about what he wants? What if I'm just some 'experience' for him?"

Lysander's response came quicker this time.

"You're assuming he doesn't already know what he wants. You're also assuming that, if he does change his mind in the future, that it would make what you're experiencing right now any less real."

Ryan blinked at his phone, feeling his throat tighten slightly.

"Ryan, I've known you a long time. You're careful with your heart, but when you love something, you love it with everything you have. And from what you're telling me, Jamie is bringing you joy, yes?"

Ryan swallowed.

"Yeah. He really is."

"Then let yourself have that joy. Yes, there's an age difference. And yes, maybe he'll grow, and maybe things will change. But that's true of any relationship. The important thing is whether you both communicate what you want and what you need from each other. Have you asked him what **he** *wants?"*

Ryan stared at the message for a long time.

No. He hadn't. He'd been so stuck in his own head, worrying about *if* Jamie was too young, *if* this was unfair, *if* it could work long-term, that he hadn't even considered that Jamie might already *know* what he wanted.

"No. I haven't asked him yet."

Lysander responded, *"Then perhaps that is your answer. Talk to him. Be honest about your concerns, but don't let fear rob you of something meaningful before it even has a chance to begin."*

Ryan let out a breath he hadn't realized he was holding.

"*You're annoyingly wise, you know that?*"

"*I do my best.*" Responded Lysander.

"Thanks, man. Seriously."

"Of course. And Ryan?"

"Yeah?"

"Something tells me Jamie already knows exactly what he wants. And it might just be you."

Ryan swallowed past the lump in his throat, staring at the words longer than necessary. His heart beat a little harder at the thought.

"Guess I'll just have to find out."

He put his phone down, scratching Max's head as the retriever mix gave him a sleepy yawn. The worry was still there, but Lysander was right—he wouldn't let it drown out the excitement bubbling beneath it.

Tomorrow, he'd talk to Jamie. And maybe, just maybe, he'd let himself believe that this thing between them could really be something.

Chapter 9

RYAN blinked awake, sunlight spilling lazily through the blinds, casting golden streaks across his sheets. His mind was groggy, but his body moved on instinct—pawing around for his phone before he even sat up. Max, still curled up at the foot of the bed, let out a sleepy sigh as Ryan grabbed his device and unlocked the screen.

The first thing he checked was his messages, his heart giving a small, eager thump as he saw Jamie's name at the top.

Jamie had sent a GIF of a cat cuddling another cat.

Ryan let out a small, breathy chuckle, his tail giving a lazy wag against the bed. *This boy.* He swiped his thumb over the screen, staring at the affectionate little animation. The way the second cat leaned into the first, seeking warmth, seeking closeness—it was so simple, so *Jamie.*

He felt warmth bloom in his chest, that same feeling he'd been carrying since last night—the soft, glowing certainty that he liked this boy, really liked him. Maybe even more than he was willing to admit to himself yet.

But then, like a shadow creeping in at the edges of his happiness, the thought returned: the age gap.

Ryan sighed, rubbing a paw over his face as he flopped back

onto the pillow, phone resting against his chest. He wanted to just let himself be happy, to ride the high of Jamie's messages and the lingering feeling of their kiss. But his mind wouldn't let him off that easy.

Jamie was twenty-one. Fresh into his twenties, barely stepping into full-fledged adulthood. Ryan was twenty-seven—still young, sure, but he'd already been through so much. He'd lived in denial, forced himself into a relationship that was never going to work, built and then unraveled the version of himself he thought the world needed him to be. He'd spent years figuring out who he was.

And Jamie? He was still starting that journey.

Ryan exhaled through his nose, staring at the ceiling. *What if I'm putting him in something too serious, too fast? he wondered. What if he wakes up one day and realizes he wants something different? Someone closer to his age, someone who's at the same place in life?*

But then another thought pushed its way in, quieter but just as persistent: *What if I'm overthinking this? What if Jamie already knows what he wants? What if I just talk to him and find out instead of spiraling alone in my bed like an idiot?*

Ryan groaned, rolling over onto his stomach and shoving his face into his pillow. "Why am I like this, Max?" he mumbled against the fabric.

The dog, half-asleep, only let out a soft huff.

Ryan pulled the phone back up, staring at Jamie's message again. The cat cuddling the other cat. Sweet, affectionate, simple. No hesitation, no fear—just warmth.

Jamie liked him. He knew that much. And maybe, just maybe, Jamie already had answers Ryan was too scared to assume.

He took a deep breath, stretching out before finally sitting up. He'd talk to Jamie. Not now—not first thing in the morning—but soon. When the moment felt right.

For now, he let himself smile again, thumbs tapping against his screen.

Ryan sent a GIF of a golden retriever flopping onto another dog. *"Mornin', pawsniper. Cuddles accepted."*

Baby steps. He could figure out the rest later. He jumped and let out a small yawn howl. Heading to the bathroom to get washed up.

As Ryan stretched and lazily scratched at his fluffy chest, his phone buzzed again. He glanced down, expecting another cute GIF or morning greeting from Jamie, but instead, he saw a new message that made his ears perk up.

"I see you went on a little liking spree on my Barkstergram last night." [GIF of a blushing anime character hiding their face]

Ryan's tail gave a small thump against the bed as he realized what Jamie was talking about. "Shit, did I go overboard?" He had spent a solid chunk of last night scrolling through Jamie's profile, liking posts about his favorite indie albums, late-night coffee musings, and candid shots of game tournaments. He hadn't even realized how many he'd tapped until now.

But then another message popped up:

"Not that I'm complaining or anything…just didn't expect it. Then I checked your page and…" A GIF of a cartoon character sweating nervously popping up.

Ryan chuckled, leaning back against his pillows. Right, Jamie had seen his posts too. His Barkstergram wasn't exactly a gold mine of personal details, but it did have snapshots of his life—gym selfies, Max sprawled out in ridiculous sleeping positions, and the occasional group shot with Bandaid and Lysander where they were either flexing or making stupid faces.

Ryan grinned and fired back a response.

"Guilty. Figured I should do my research on the guy I kissed last night. [smirking emoji]"

Jamie's typing bubbles appeared, disappeared, then came back again.

"Oh my god, Ryan." A GIF of someone dramatically fainting followed it.

Ryan snickered, imagining Jamie hiding his face behind his paws in embarrassment. He liked this—seeing Jamie's flustered reactions, the way he got shy even through texts. It was endearing.

"Relax, pawsniper. You looked through mine too, huh? See anything you like? [winking emoji]"

There was another pause before Jamie sent a single message that made Ryan's heart do a weird little flip.

"Yeah...I did."

Ryan stared at the words, his goofy grin softening into something fonder. The warmth in his chest only grew, and the worries about their age difference faded into the background.

This was real. This was nice.

And maybe, just maybe, it was exactly what Ryan needed. Ryan flopped onto the couch, phone in hand, his heart thumping with a mix of excitement and nerves. He and Jamie had exchanged a flurry of playful messages about Barkstergram posts, but the age gap hung in the back of Ryan's mind like a nagging reminder. He steeled himself, took a breath, and typed:

"Hey, so...can I ask you something kinda awkward?"

The typing bubbles popped up almost immediately.

"Sure, shoot."

Ryan swallowed, staring at the screen. *You can do this*, he told himself.

"It's about our ages. I just...noticed you're 21. I'm 27. How do you feel about that? Is it...weird?"

He hit send, exhaling shakily. A short pause followed. Ryan could practically feel the tension in the silence. Then the phone buzzed:

"I figured you might bring that up eventually. Tbh, I don't see it as a big issue. So long as someone isn't younger than me, I'm not too concerned about the gap. [nervous laugh emoji]"

Ryan felt a small wave of relief wash over him, but still typed carefully:

"I guess I was just worried. It's not a huge gap, but we're at different points in our lives."

Again, a pause as Jamie composed his thoughts:

"I mean, sure. But everyone's at different points. Doesn't matter if you're 27 or 37, you know? It's about how we connect right now. And...I kind of like that you're older."

Ryan blinked, the corners of his mouth curving into a surprised smile. *He likes that I'm older?*

"Yeah?"

"Yeah...I guess it's kind of nice. You've lived a bit, you've seen more. I feel like I can trust you to...guide me a bit? That probably sounds weird, sorry."

Ryan's tail gave a wag against the couch cushion, his cheeks warming at the honesty in Jamie's words. He typed back softly:

"Nah, it doesn't sound weird. I like...being someone you can trust. And we can figure out this "different points in life" thing as we go."

"Exactly. I don't want age to be the reason we don't at least see where this goes."

Ryan let out a breath he hadn't realized he was holding. The knot in his chest loosened as he read and reread Jamie's reply. For the first time in days, the tension about the age gap finally seemed to ebb.

"Thanks for being honest. You have no idea how relieved I am to hear you say all that."

A new message popped up in reply:

"Anytime. Now stop worrying. And let's make sure we're free to hang out again soon. No excuses, old man." [winking emoji]

Ryan couldn't help but grin at that. He leaned his head back against the couch, heart lighter than it had been in ages.

"You got it, youngster."

Jamie responded with a GIF of a cat rolling its eyes dramatically. Ryan laughed out loud. This felt good—*they* felt good. And for now, that was enough.

After sending a few more playful texts back and forth with Jamie, Ryan finally decided to shoot his shot.

"So, uh...Any interest in catching a movie this Friday? There's that new sci-fi one coming out, figured we could grab some snacks, nerd out a little, maybe get some popcorn in our fur."

Jamie's typing bubbles appeared almost instantly.

"That actually sounds really fun. But just so you know...I'm a very serious movie watcher. If you talk during the film, I will bite you."

Ryan smirked, already picturing Jamie getting all intense about it.

"Noted. I'll sit there all good and quiet like a perfect gentleman. Unless there's a really cool explosion, then I make no promises."

"I suppose I can allow one explosion reaction. Friday it is, then. [smiling emoji]"

"Can't wait. See you then, pawsniper. [winking emoji]"

Friday night arrived faster than Ryan expected. He spent the whole afternoon buzzing with restless energy, his gym session barely taking the edge off. He'd gone through *three* different outfits before settling on something effortlessly casual—nice-fitting jeans, a relaxed hoodie, and his favorite high-tops. He wanted to look good but not *too* put together. Not like he'd been agonizing over it for the past hour or anything.

Now, he was parked outside Jamie's place, fingers drumming against the steering wheel as he took a steadying breath. Max wasn't there to hype him up this time, so he had to rely on sheer confidence—or, at the very least, *pretend* he had sheer confidence.

Then the front door opened, and all thoughts flew out of his head.

Jamie stepped out wearing a dark zip-up hoodie over a graphic tee, some fitted jeans, and sneakers that had clearly seen better days but still looked effortlessly cool on him. His fur had a subtle fluff to it, like he'd brushed it out a little more than usual, and his ears twitched slightly as he locked up his house before heading toward Ryan's car.

Ryan swallowed hard, heart thumping as he watched Jamie jog up to the passenger side and slide in. "Hey," Jamie greeted, shooting him a soft smile as he clicked his seatbelt in place.

Ryan couldn't stop himself from sneaking a glance. Or three.

Jamie shifted slightly in his seat, ears flicking back as he caught Ryan *still* looking at him out of the corner of his eye. His face instantly burned. "What?" he asked, his voice small but curious, tail flicking behind him.

Ryan smirked, loving how easy it was to fluster him. "Nothing," he teased, turning his gaze back to the road. "I just think you're really cute."

Jamie made a sound that was somewhere between a scoff and an embarrassed squeak. His tail gave a little involuntary wag, and he quickly tried to smother it by shifting in his seat. "You *can't* just say that," he mumbled, rubbing the back of his neck as his face turned a deeper shade of red.

Ryan chuckled, shoulders shaking slightly. "Why not? It's true."

Jamie huffed, but his tail *definitely* wasn't stopping. After a few seconds of flustered silence, Ryan suddenly felt movement beside him. Jamie, very carefully, very *coolly*, reached over and hesitantly placed his paw over Ryan's.

Ryan's breath hitched slightly as Jamie's fingers curled gently around his own, resting there like it was something natural. The weight of it sent a warm, tingling feeling up Ryan's arm, and he glanced down at their hands for just a second before he let out a quiet chuckle, squeezing Jamie's paw in return.

"You know," Ryan mused, his ears flicking with amusement, "for someone who's all flustered about being called cute, you're out here pulling some smooth moves."

Jamie, still blushing, tightened his grip slightly but didn't let go. "Shut up and drive," he muttered, eyes fixed out the window.

Ryan grinned, his own face feeling a little warmer than before as he turned his focus back on the road. "Yes, sir," he teased, his tail wagging behind him as he gave Jamie's paw one more soft squeeze before resting it between them for the rest of the drive.

The theater was buzzing with the hum of Friday night excitement, the scent of buttery popcorn and sweet candy hanging heavy in the air. Ryan pulled into the lot, parking in a good spot before glancing over at Jamie, who was scrolling through his phone idly. The glow of the screen illuminated his face, his eyes reflecting the light, and Ryan found himself staring again.

Jamie noticed and smirked. "What, still think I'm cute?"

Ryan just grinned and leaned back in his seat. "Oh, *absolutely*."

Jamie rolled his eyes, but Ryan didn't miss the flicker of pink across his cheeks as they stepped out of the car. The movie posters lined the glass walls of the entrance, glowing under the neon marquee lights. Ryan held the door open for Jamie, who muttered a small "thanks" before walking in, eyes scanning the rows of movie posters.

Ryan led them straight to the ticket counter, stepping forward confidently. "Two for 'Blood Moon Manor,'" he said, sliding his card across the counter before Jamie could even *think* about reaching for his wallet.

Jamie's ears perked in protest. "Ryan, I could've—"

Ryan cut him off with a smug grin. "You could've, but you didn't."

Jamie gave him a half-hearted glare, crossing his arms, but Ryan could see the tiniest upward twitch at the corners of his lips.

Next stop: the concession stand. The glass cases displayed rows of freshly popped popcorn, shiny-wrapped candies, and perfectly chilled sodas. Ryan glanced at Jamie, who was still looking at the menu overhead, eyes flicking between the choices.

"What are you thinking?" Ryan asked innocently.

Jamie hummed. "Maybe just a popcorn and a drink. Oh, and those sour gummies—"

Ryan nodded thoughtfully, then turned to the cashier. "Yeah, we'll take the biggest popcorn you got, *two* drinks, the sour gummies *and* those chocolate-covered pretzels. Oh, and a pack of those caramel chews." He slid his card across the counter before Jamie even realized what was happening.

Jamie blinked in horror. "Ryan!"

Ryan grinned, leaning against the counter. "What? You wanted snacks, I *got* you snacks."

Jamie crossed his arms, giving him a playful, angry pout. "You *tricked* me."

Ryan winked. "I *strategized*."

Jamie huffed dramatically, but his tail gave away the fact that he wasn't actually mad. He took his drink from Ryan begrudgingly as they headed toward the theater. "This is a *conspiracy*," he muttered.

"You're just mad I'm a *generous and thoughtful* date," Ryan teased, nudging him with his elbow.

Jamie scoffed, but his ears flicked downward in a flustered way as they found their seats. The theater was dimly lit, a few previews already rolling on screen. Ryan made sure to grab seats in a good row—centered, not too close but not too far back.

The moment the lights dimmed completely, the atmosphere shifted. The heavy, eerie score of the movie set in, immediately raising the tension in the room. Ryan popped a handful of popcorn into his mouth, chewing slowly, but his focus wasn't entirely on the movie—not when Jamie was sitting *right there*, sipping on his drink quietly, his tail occasionally brushing Ryan's leg under the armrest.

Ryan wanted to hold Jamie's paw.

The thought came so naturally it almost startled him. His own fingers twitched in his lap, torn between reaching out and hesitating. It wasn't just that he *wanted* to—it was that they were *in public*. He hadn't been openly affectionate with someone like this before. What if people stared? What if it felt *too* obvious?

Jamie, seemingly noticing Ryan's sudden tension, glanced at him. His golden eyes, reflecting the flickering light of the screen, searched Ryan's face for a moment before he smirked softly.

"Scared already?" he whispered teasingly.

Ryan huffed, forcing himself to relax. "No."

Jamie giggled quietly, clearly unconvinced. Then, after a brief pause, he slowly leaned in, resting his head lightly on Ryan's shoulder.

Ryan felt his heart *stop*.

Jamie was *right there*, his warmth radiating through Ryan's hoodie, his scent—a mix of something faintly sweet and a little earthy—wrapping around Ryan in a way that made his chest ache. Ryan swallowed hard, his fingers twitching again.

Screw it.

He slowly, cautiously shifted his hand toward Jamie's, barely grazing the tips of his fingers against Jamie's palm.

Jamie's tail flicked. Then, before Ryan could second-guess himself, Jamie's fingers curled around his, warm and steady.

Ryan felt like his entire body *exhaled* at once.

They stayed like that as the movie progressed, though it wasn't long before Ryan regretted picking something *scary* for their first movie date.

The film was *way* more intense than he'd anticipated.

At one particularly horrifying moment—a long, suspenseful silence followed by a *brutal* jump scare—Ryan flinched, gripping the armrest with his free paw.

Jamie? Jamie just *giggled.*

Ryan turned to him, wide-eyed. "You're *laughing*?" he whispered.

Jamie covered his mouth to stifle more giggles. "You jumped so hard," he whispered back, his tail wagging behind him.

Ryan scowled playfully. "It was *unexpected.*"

Jamie poked him in the side. "I thought you were *tough, big guy.*"

Ryan groaned, rolling his eyes. "Yeah, yeah, laugh it up, pawsniper."

And Jamie *did*—softly, endearingly, his head still resting against Ryan's shoulder like it was the most natural place to be.

By the time the credits rolled, Ryan realized the weight against him had grown heavier.

Jamie had fallen asleep.

Ryan blinked, looking down at him, a wave of tenderness washing over him. Jamie's breathing was slow and steady, his paw still resting loosely in Ryan's. The dim glow of the screen cast soft shadows over his fur, highlighting the gentle rise and fall of his chest.

Ryan didn't want to wake him.

For the first time in a long, long while, he felt completely at peace. No nagging doubts, no overthinking—just warmth, quiet, and the soft press of someone he cared about against him.

But eventually, the theater began emptying out, and Ryan sighed, knowing they had to go.

He gently nudged Jamie's paw. "Hey, sleepyhead," he murmured.

Jamie made a soft noise in protest, shifting slightly but not opening his eyes.

Ryan huffed a quiet laugh. "C'mon, the movie's over. Unless you wanna be that guy who gets kicked out by the cleaning crew."

Jamie finally stirred, blinking blearily up at him. "Mmm... we made it?"

Ryan smirked. "I did. You passed out, champ."

Jamie groaned, rubbing his face. "Ugh. That's so embarrassing."

Ryan squeezed his paw before letting go. "Nah, it was kinda cute."

Jamie shot him a sleepy glare. "You can't just keep calling me cute."

Ryan grinned as they stood, stretching. "I absolutely can."

Jamie rolled his eyes, but his tail gave a small wag as they made their way out of the theater, stepping into the cool night air together. The world felt a little quieter, a little softer, and Ryan?

He felt happy.

As they stepped out of the theater and into the crisp night air, Ryan stole another glance at Jamie. The striped hyena looked up at him, a sleepy but content smile tugging at the corners of his muzzle. His golden eyes gleamed under the streetlights, and for a moment, Ryan was completely lost in them.

They walked side by side toward Ryan's car, their bodies close but not quite touching. The whole night had been perfect—better than perfect. Ryan's chest still buzzed with warmth from their time together, from the way Jamie had leaned into him during the movie, from the feeling of his hand in his own.

Just as they stepped into the near-empty parking lot, Jamie's ears suddenly flicked backward. His entire body stiffened. His face twisted from relaxed happiness into something sharp, something fearful.

Ryan barely had time to register it before Jamie sucked in a sharp breath, eyes going wide in terror. "Ryan, look out!"

The warning barely left Jamie's lips before a brutal *thud* cracked against the side of Ryan's skull.

Pain exploded in his head—sharp, blinding, white-hot. His vision blurred instantly, a searing wave of dizziness crashing over him as his knees buckled beneath him. The world tilted violently, and before he could process what was happening, he was on the ground.

His body hit the pavement with a heavy, disoriented thump. The cold concrete bit into his palms as he instinctively tried to push himself up, but his limbs felt unresponsive, sluggish. His ears rang, a high-pitched whine drowning out the distant sound of Jamie's panicked voice.

His mind struggled to catch up, to make sense of what had just happened. One second, he had been walking to the car. The next, the entire world had tilted—his vision darkening at the edges, pain throbbing violently behind his eyes.

He forced himself to blink, to focus.

Jamie was kneeling beside him, his face stricken with panic, his paws trembling as they hovered over Ryan's shoulders like he didn't know whether to touch him or not. His mouth was moving, but Ryan couldn't hear the words over the relentless ringing in his skull.

Then, from the corner of his blurred vision, Ryan saw movement. A figure standing over them.

Ryan's pulse slammed against his ribs. Someone was still there.

Jamie's head snapped up toward them, his ears flattened, his body shifting instinctively in front of Ryan like a shield. His entire posture screamed fear, but also something protective.

Ryan gritted his teeth, forcing himself to move, his fingers curling against the pavement. His body screamed in protest, his head swimming with nausea, but he fought through it, his instincts roaring one single command in his dazed mind:

Get up.

Chapter 10

RYAN'S vision swam as he forced himself to his feet, blood trickling hot and sticky down his temple, matting into his fur. His head throbbed, nausea creeping into his stomach, but none of that mattered—not when Jamie was behind him, trembling, ears pinned back in fear.

His instincts took over.

He stepped in front of Jamie, chest heaving, legs unsteady but firm, his entire body screaming one message loud and clear: *You will not touch him.*

A low, primal growl rumbled from Ryan's throat as his unfocused gaze locked onto the figure before him—a red wolf, pacing back and forth under the dim glow of the streetlights, gripping a metal pipe in his paw like he was waiting for the right moment to strike again. His fur bristled, sharp amber eyes gleaming with something sick and twisted. A sneer twisted his muzzle.

"Fucking finally," the wolf spat, his voice dripping with venom. "I knew I'd find you sooner or later, Jamie. You no-good whore."

Jamie stiffened behind Ryan, his breath hitching in horror. "What the fuck is wrong with you, Zack?!" he shouted, voice trembling with a mixture of fury and fear.

Zack let out a sharp, humorless laugh, rolling the pipe between his fingers. His tail lashed, his sneer deepening. "What's wrong with *me*?" He gestured wildly, teeth flashing. "What's wrong is seeing you all cozied up with some half-breed dog, opening your legs like the little slut I always knew you were."

Ryan barely registered the words before a white-hot rage surged through him, a snarl ripping from his throat.

He lunged.

The force of his tackle sent Zack crashing onto the pavement with a dull, brutal *thud*. The metal pipe clattered against the asphalt as Ryan's weight bore down on him, fists already flying. The impact sent a jolt of pain through Ryan's already bruised skull, but he didn't care.

He would make this bastard regret every single word.

Zack grunted as Ryan's first punch connected, snapping his head to the side, but he recovered quickly. With a growl, he swung wildly, claws scraping against Ryan's side as he tried to force him off. Ryan snarled, grabbing Zack's wrist and twisting it hard, using the leverage to roll them over, straddling Zack's chest.

He swung again. Knuckles collided against bone. Another hit. Zack let out a choked curse, writhing beneath him, but Ryan kept him pinned, his rage unrelenting.

"Ryan, stop!" Jamie's voice cut through the chaos, pleading.

But Zack took advantage of the distraction.

With a snarl, he shoved his knee up into Ryan's stomach, the impact knocking the breath out of him for a split second—just long enough for Zack to shove him off. Ryan hit the pavement hard, rolling onto his side just as Zack scrambled to his feet, grabbing the metal pipe again with shaking hands.

Ryan was already pushing himself up, blood dripping from his muzzle, but before either of them could make another move—

Headlights sliced through the night.

A sleek, black car screeched to a halt nearby. The doors flew open.

Ryan barely had time to react before two men rushed out, their footfalls pounding against the pavement.

"Jamie, run!" Ryan shouted, but it was too late.

One of them—a tall, lanky coyote—grabbed Jamie's arm, wrenching him backward. Jamie yelped, struggling, kicking out wildly. Another man, a massive bull of a wolf, seized Jamie's other arm, the two dragging him toward the car.

"No! Get off me!" Jamie screamed, thrashing desperately. His claws dug into one of their arms, but the wolf simply snarled and yanked harder, nearly lifting Jamie off his feet.

Ryan saw red.

He tried to lunge toward Jamie, but Zack was faster—swinging the pipe straight into Ryan's ribs.

The impact sent an explosion of pain through Ryan's body, forcing him to his knees with a strangled gasp. He barely had time to recover before another pair of hands grabbed him from behind.

Another man—one Ryan hadn't even seen—wrapped his arms around Ryan's torso in a crushing grip, locking his arms in place. Ryan roared, trying to break free, but Zack was already on him, slamming his fist into Ryan's face.

Then another.

And another.

Pain burst across his skull, each strike rattling his senses. His vision blurred, dark spots creeping in at the edges. He struggled against the hold keeping him trapped, but his body was weakening, his limbs sluggish and heavy.

"Ryan!" Jamie's voice cracked, full of terror, but it was growing distant, like he was being pulled away—

Ryan forced his eyes open. Through the haze of blood and pain, he saw Jamie still fighting, still kicking, his golden eyes wide with fear as the men forced him into the back seat of the car.

Ryan reached for him.

"Jamie—!"

But then another blow came, this one to the back of his head.

The world tilted.

Sound became muffled. His body went numb.

The last thing he saw was Jamie's tear-streaked face, his arms outstretched toward Ryan even as the car door slammed shut between them.

Then everything faded to black.

Darkness faded into warmth.

The soft chirping of birds filled the air, mingling with the whisper of wind through the tall trees. Ryan stood in the middle of a beautiful forest, the sunlight filtering through the green canopy, dappling the ground in golden patches. The scent of damp earth and fresh blossoms surrounded him, crisp and full of life.

Beside him, Jamie walked with that small, shy smile that always made Ryan's chest ache in the best way. His golden eyes sparkled in the afternoon light, his tail swaying lazily as they strolled down the winding dirt path. The trees around them seemed to hum with peace, swaying gently in the wind, their leaves whispering secrets.

Ryan reached out, wrapping his arm around Jamie's waist, pulling him close. He could feel the warmth of him—solid, real. Jamie let out a small, content sigh, leaning into him, his muzzle nestled against Ryan's shoulder.

Ryan tilted his head down, breathing him in. "You're so warm," he murmured.

Jamie chuckled softly, his fingers curling into Ryan's hoodie. "Of course I am. You always say that."

Ryan smiled, brushing his nose against Jamie's fur. The moment felt perfect. *Peaceful.*

But then—something shifted.

Jamie's voice became distant, like an echo rippling through water. "Ryan..."

Ryan blinked. His fingers twitched against Jamie's side.

"Ryan..." Jamie's voice came again, but this time, it wasn't dreamy or soft. It was urgent. *Pleading.*

Ryan's brow furrowed as Jamie's form seemed to blur, his golden eyes filled with something desperate. "Ryan..."

Then—darkness.

Ryan's breath hitched as he jolted awake, a sharp, sterile scent filling his nostrils. Fluorescent lights buzzed faintly overhead. His body ached, throbbing from head to toe, the weight of reality crashing down on him in an instant.

And then he heard it—his name.

"Ryan," came a voice, steady, *familiar.*

Ryan's bleary eyes snapped toward the source, confusion swirling in his still-dazed mind. Sam sat beside him, leaning forward, concern etched deeply into his face. Behind him, Bandaid and Lysander stood, their normally strong, confident postures replaced with something fragile. Bandaid's cheeks were damp with tear streaks, his paws gripping onto Lysander's arm as if to steady himself. Lysander's expression was tense, his usually composed demeanor cracked with worry.

Ryan's vision swam. His throat felt raw as he croaked, "Sam...?"

Sam's face softened, his same gentle, familiar warmth still present after all this time. "Yeah, Ry, it's me," he said, voice steady but thick with emotion.

Ryan's gaze darted around the unfamiliar white room—IVs, heart monitor, hospital walls. But none of it mattered. His eyes widened, and in an instant, it all came rushing back.

The parking lot.

The red wolf.

The pipe.

The fight.

The black car.

His entire body seized as a new kind of pain ripped through him.

"Jamie!" he choked out, his heart slamming against his ribs.

He tried to sit up, ignoring the searing agony that shot through his limbs. He barely got halfway before strong hands pushed him back down—Sam's, firm but careful.

"Ryan, *stop*!" Sam pleaded, his grip tightening.

"Get off me!" Ryan snarled, panic overriding reason. He struggled against them, raw desperation consuming him. Bandaid sobbed as he stepped in, pressing down on Ryan's shoulder to help Sam restrain him, tears spilling freely from his wide eyes.

"Ryan, *please*!" Bandaid cried, his voice cracking. "Stop! You're gonna hurt yourself!"

Lysander stood rigid, his fists clenched, his ears pinned back in grief, but his touch was gentle as he helped hold Ryan's other arm down. "You need to calm yourself," he said, voice unusually unsteady.

Ryan's breaths were ragged, his body still fighting, but then he saw it. The fear in their eyes. The sheer helplessness written across their faces.

Bandaid was crying. Lysander looked shaken. Sam—Sam looked *broken*.

Ryan stilled.

His chest rose and fell in uneven bursts as his brain tried to catch up. His paws clenched into the hospital sheets.

"Where is he?" Ryan's voice was hoarse, but this time, it was stern. Unrelenting. He searched their faces, his stomach twisting into knots. "Where is Jamie?"

Silence.

The three of them exchanged glances, a shared grief settling between them. Bandaid bit his lip, fresh tears spilling. Lysander lowered his gaze.

Sam closed his eyes for a long, steadying breath before looking back at Ryan, his expression unreadable.

Ryan's stomach dropped.

His heart pounded.

"Sam," Ryan rasped, his body trembling with adrenaline and exhaustion. "Where is he?"

Sam took a slow breath, clearly choosing his words carefully as he leaned forward. His eyes, warm but heavy with exhaustion, locked onto Ryan's.

"Ryan...you've been out for three days."

Ryan's breath caught in his throat.

"You were brought in barely alive," Sam continued, voice steady but tinged with emotion. "The damage was bad, but somehow, nothing was life-threatening. You've got broken ribs, deep bruising all over your torso, a concussion—" His eyes flickered to the side of Ryan's head, "—and you needed stitches where that bastard hit you with the pipe."

Ryan instinctively reached up, fingers grazing over the side of his skull. Beneath the bandages, he could feel the tenderness of healing wounds, the slight sting where the stitches pulled against his fur. His whole body ached—his limbs felt heavier than they should, his chest tight with every breath. He hadn't even realized how much pain he was in until now.

But none of that mattered.

His jaw clenched as his mind snapped back to Jamie.

Sam hesitated, exchanging a look with Lysander and Bandaid. "The police found Jamie the next day," he said, his voice quieter now.

Ryan's stomach twisted violently. His grip on the hospital sheets tightened. "Where?" he rasped.

Sam swallowed, his expression unreadable. "He was

slumped over on the pier," he said carefully. "Barely conscious when they got to him."

Ryan's whole body tensed, heat rising in his chest.

"He has a broken wrist," Sam continued, his voice controlled but careful, "deep contusions all over his body, and—" He exhaled sharply. "—he still hasn't woken up. He's in a stable condition, but he's comatose. They've got him in the ICU."

Ryan stared straight ahead, his expression unreadable, but tears spilled silently down his face, hot and unchecked. His chest burned—not just with grief, but rage. His ears rang, Sam's words twisting over and over in his mind.

Jamie. *Beaten.* Left on a pier like trash. Unconscious for three days.

Ryan's fingers clenched into the sheets, knuckles whitening as the fire inside him raged higher. The image of Jamie's small, exhausted smile before they reached the car played in his mind, overlapping with the sight of him being dragged away, fighting, crying out—

Ryan let out a shaky breath. His head ached, his ribs screamed, but none of it compared to the sheer fury gripping his soul.

The boy he loved had been hurt.

And all Ryan could do was lie there.

The beeping of the heart monitor beside him quickened, but Ryan barely registered it.

Bandaid sniffled, his grip on Ryan's arm tightening, voice breaking as he whispered, "I-I know you're mad, Ry...but you gotta breathe."

Lysander's paw landed on Ryan's shoulder, grounding, solid. "Jamie's still here," he said carefully. "And when he wakes up, he's going to need you."

Ryan shut his eyes, forcing himself to swallow down the molten anger threatening to consume him.

Jamie *needed* him. That was the only thing that mattered

now.

With a slow, ragged breath, Ryan opened his eyes and, with quiet, steely determination, said,

"I need to see him."

Sam held Ryan's gaze, the steady warmth in his eyes unwavering. "As soon as the doctor clears you, we'll all go see him," he promised, voice firm but gentle.

Ryan swallowed, nodding slightly, but the burning in his chest only grew. His fingers clenched into the thin hospital blanket as the fire inside him reignited. His jaw tightened, and he spat out the question that had been clawing at his throat.

"Did they find Zack?" His voice was raw, laced with barely restrained fury. "And the rest of those bastards?"

Sam let out a slow breath, exchanging a look with Bandaid and Lysander before answering carefully. "The police are still investigating," he admitted. "They have all the footage from the theater and the pier. They found the vehicle, and..." He hesitated, eyes darkening. "They got one of the wolves. He's being held while they work on tracking down the others."

Ryan's chest heaved, the world around him blurring as the rage twisted with something even worse—*guilt*.

His fists trembled. His whole body tensed as fresh tears slipped down his face, unchecked. "I found him," he choked, voice shaking. "I found what I was looking for. Someone who makes me feel whole, someone who makes me—" He gasped, unable to finish the sentence. "And now it's being ripped away from me like some kind of fucking punishment."

Sam's face remained heartbreakingly kind as he reached out, cupping Ryan's head between his hands, pressing their foreheads together. "Ryan," he murmured, voice soft but firm. "The world doesn't punish us for love."

Ryan let out a shuddering breath, but Sam continued, his thumbs brushing against Ryan's temples in soothing circles. "Sometimes bad things happen to the most beautiful and good people. And it's unfair. But that doesn't mean love wasn't meant for you. It doesn't mean this is a punishment."

Ryan trembled, his breath coming out in uneven, ragged bursts. "But Jamie—"

Sam pulled back just enough to meet his eyes. "Jamie's still here," he said, voice steady. "He needs you, Ryan. And I know you—you're not gonna let him face this alone."

Ryan sniffled, his body slowly unwinding under Sam's touch. His heart still ached, the weight of everything pressing down on him, but Sam was right. Jamie needed him.

Sam gave a small nod to the others before standing and stepping out to grab the doctor. Bandaid wiped at his face with his hoodie sleeve, sniffling as he patted Ryan's arm. "You scared the shit out of us, man," he murmured. Lysander nodded, his own expression tight with something unreadable, but his eyes held nothing but care.

After a brief conversation with the doctor, Ryan was finally cleared to leave his hospital bed. Every inch of his body hurt, but he didn't care. His steps were slow, stiff, but determined as he followed Sam, Bandaid, and Lysander down the hall toward the ICU.

When they arrived at Jamie's room, Ryan hesitated for just a moment, his breath catching in his throat.

Then he stepped inside.

Jamie lay still against the pristine white sheets, his fur marked with bruises, his wrist wrapped tightly in a cast. The sight of him—so small in the vastness of the hospital bed—made Ryan's stomach churn. His chest ached so deeply that he thought he might crumble under the weight of it.

Bandaid and Lysander stopped at the doorway, watching carefully as Ryan moved forward. His legs felt weak, his body screaming at him to rest, but nothing could stop him from getting closer.

He sat beside Jamie's bed, staring at him, taking in every

rise and fall of his chest, every gentle flicker of his closed eyelids. Slowly, shakily, Ryan reached out, taking Jamie's paw in his own. His thumb brushed along Jamie's fingers, tracing the familiar warmth he thought he might never feel again.

The moment the realization truly hit him—that Jamie had been beaten, that he had suffered alone—a sob tore through Ryan's throat. He hunched forward, pressing Jamie's paw against his forehead as his body broke.

"I'm so sorry," he whispered, his voice cracking. "I'm so—so sorry."

His tears soaked into the sheets, his sobs shaking his already battered body, but he couldn't stop. The pain in his heart was unbearable. He clutched Jamie's paw tighter, pressing his forehead against his lover's chest, whispering apologies over and over again.

Then—soft, warm hands settled onto his back.

Bandaid. Lysander. Sam.

One by one, they stepped forward, wrapping their arms around him. Bandaid was still crying, his sniffling uneven as he buried his face into Ryan's shoulder. Lysander, quiet and composed but there, resting a steadying hand on Ryan's back. Sam, holding Ryan's arm, grounding him as Ryan sobbed into Jamie's chest.

Ryan clenched his eyes shut, his grip on Jamie tightening. His body trembled beneath the weight of it all, but through the grief, through the tears, he forced himself to speak.

His voice, broken and raw, barely a whisper.

"I, uh..." He sniffled, breath hitching as he struggled to get the words out. "I wrote you something, I was gonna read it like some sap when we got back to your house." He let out a chuckling sob.

The others stayed quiet, still holding onto him, as he gathered his breath, his words coming through the tears.

"*I met a boy, he's kind, and when he smiles, his forehead crinkles in the sweetest way."*

Ryan swallowed, his voice cracking.

"*A smile that spreads when he laughs, causing my heart to swell; a wave crashing on the shore followed by a calming backwash.*"

His grip on Jamie's paw tightened.

"*When I catch his stare, I can't help but burn crimson and give him a goofy grin, one that he says drives him wild.*"

He let out a trembling breath, his forehead still pressed against Jamie's chest.

"*Little does he know that when he says that, my broken heart starts to mend. A flower blooming in a crack in the pavement.*"

Bandaid sniffled, his grip on Ryan tightening.

"*I know this is new, but he makes it feėl so easy. Passion from your gaze inspires me to feel love again. A natural love that defies logic, for love is wild.*"

Ryan swallowed hard, his fingers trembling.

"*Wild like the grin on my face, but also kind like this boy is to me.*"

His tears dripped onto Jamie's sheets as he whispered the final words.

"*I met a boy, and I am wild about him.*"

Silence filled the room, heavy and aching.

Ryan closed his eyes, his breath shaky as he held onto Jamie like he was the most fragile, precious thing in the world.

Please, please wake up, he begged silently.

Please come back to me.

The night carried on in quiet stillness, the rhythmic beeping of Jamie's monitors the only sound filling the dimly lit hospital room. After some time, Bandaid, Lysander, and Sam exchanged weary looks before realizing Ryan wasn't moving from his spot.

"You're staying, huh?" Bandaid asked softly, wiping at his tired eyes.

Ryan just nodded, still gripping Jamie's paw, his thumb

idly brushing over his fingers.

Lysander let out a quiet sigh, placing a firm paw on Ryan's shoulder. "We'll be back in the morning," he said, voice steady. "Try to get some rest."

Bandaid hesitated before stepping forward and wrapping his arms around Ryan in a tight, warm hug. "Don't be afraid to text us, okay?" he murmured, voice thick with emotion.

Ryan nodded against his shoulder before Bandaid finally pulled away, rubbing at his face with his sleeve. Sam gave Ryan a lingering look, as if trying to say a million things without speaking, then simply gave a firm nod before following the others out.

Ryan was alone with Jamie again.

For the next few hours, he sat at his bedside, watching him breathe, adjusting his blankets, murmuring soft words of reassurance even if Jamie couldn't hear them. When the nurses came in to check on Jamie, Ryan made sure to smile at them, thanking them for their care. He helped where he could—fetching ice chips, adjusting pillows, anything to feel like he was doing something.

The staff quickly took notice of him.

By the second night, one of the nurses—a soft-spoken Labrador—brought in a small pillow and an extra blanket, setting it on the couch.

"For you," she said gently. "You've been here for nearly two days straight. If you're staying, you should at least be comfortable."

Ryan hesitated, then murmured a quiet, "Thank you."

Over the next week, Ryan barely left Jamie's side. The hospital staff grew accustomed to his presence, occasionally reminding him to eat or drink something. Lysander stopped by often, bringing clean clothes and setting them down with a quiet insistence that Ryan change.

On the seventh night, Lysander arrived once more, carrying a fresh duffel bag. This time, however, he didn't just leave the clothes and go. Instead, he sat down beside Ryan, folding his arms as he studied him.

"You need to go home," Lysander finally said.

Ryan's ears twitched, but he didn't look up. "I'm fine," he muttered, fingers idly brushing over Jamie's paw again.

Lysander let out a slow breath. "Ryan."

Ryan clenched his jaw, but Lysander wasn't backing down.

"You haven't left this hospital since you woke up. Max needs you. You need to rest." His voice softened, the usual firm cadence shifting into something quieter. "Jamie wouldn't want you to run yourself into the ground."

Ryan swallowed hard, the weight of his exhaustion pressing into him all at once.

Lysander gave him a moment before standing up, reaching out and pulling Ryan into a firm, grounding hug. "Go home," he murmured. "Just for a night."

Ryan squeezed his eyes shut before finally nodding against his friend's shoulder.

That night, after calling work and securing a few weeks off, Ryan finally stepped out of the hospital for the first time in days.

The drive home felt strange—almost hollow. The second he stepped through the front door, a familiar blur of golden fur came bounding toward him.

"Max," Ryan breathed, sinking to the floor as his dog buried his face into Ryan's chest, whining, tail wagging furiously.

Ryan wrapped his arms around him, pressing his face into Max's fur. "I missed you too, bud."

After giving Max some much-needed attention, Ryan shuffled into his bedroom. He felt heavy, drained, his mind teetering between exhaustion and an endless swirl of thoughts. As he kicked off his shoes and emptied his pockets onto the nightstand, a small slip of paper fluttered to the floor.

He bent down, picking it up.

It was the receipt from the movie theater.

Ryan's fingers trembled as he stared at it. A simple piece of paper, but it held so much more than inked numbers and transaction details.

It was *their* night. Their perfect night. The last time Jamie had smiled, laughed, teased him about being scared.

His vision blurred, his grip tightening on the paper.

He needed Jamie to be okay.

He needed him to wake up.

As he sat on the edge of the bed, staring at the small receipt in his hands, the warmth in his chest was quickly overtaken by something colder.

Zack.

Ryan's jaw tightened, his ears pressing back as rage pulsed through his veins.

He grabbed his phone, quickly opening a search engine. His fingers moved with purpose, typing out a name that burned like fire on his tongue.

Zack—Red Wolf—Assault—Theater Incident

If the police weren't going to find him fast enough...

Then Ryan would find him *himself.*

Chapter 11

RYAN scrolled through article after article, his vision narrowing with each word.

There wasn't much—the police were still investigating, and most of the reports were vague. The only solid lead was a recent court date for one of the assailants who had been caught. *Released on bond.*

Ryan's blood boiled.

The guy had walked free. After what they did to Jamie.

His paws clenched against his phone as he kept digging, searching the name tied to the case. He found it linked to a Barkstergram account—wide open, full of careless posts, the guy clearly not thinking twice about keeping a low profile.

Ryan scrolled through his pictures, noting the geotags. A local bar—Talon's Edge—kept popping up over and over. The same bar. The same stupid poses with drinks in hand, like he had nothing to worry about.

Ryan's lip curled.

He grabbed his jacket, pulling it on quickly. He didn't even think about texting Lysander or Bandaid. This wasn't something he was going to talk about.

This was something he was going to handle.

The neon lights of Talon's Edge buzzed softly in the night, flickering against the wet pavement from a light drizzle earlier that evening. Ryan parked across the street, sitting in his car for a moment, watching the entrance.

Then he saw him.

The other wolf from the article. The one who had been *there* that night.

Ryan's breath came slow and measured as he watched the guy leave the bar, stumbling slightly, muttering something to a friend before waving them off and heading toward his apartment alone.

Ryan followed.

He kept a safe distance, his hands clenched in his jacket pockets, eyes locked onto his target. The wolf moved lazily through the streets, completely unaware of Ryan trailing behind him.

When he reached his apartment, Ryan watched him unlock the building's glass door, stepping inside.

Now.

Ryan surged forward, slipping in before the door could fully shut.

Before the wolf could react, Ryan grabbed him, spinning him around and slamming him against the glass.

The impact rattled the door. The wolf let out a startled gasp, his paws coming up defensively, his reflection wide-eyed with shock.

"Wha—What the fuck?!" He struggled, but Ryan pressed him harder against the glass, his larger frame pinning him easily.

Ryan's voice was low, dangerous. "Where's Zack?"

The wolf's breathing was erratic, his ears pinned flat. "I—I don't know, man! I don't—"

Ryan growled, pressing his forearm harder against the wolf's chest. "Don't lie to me."

The guy's breath hitched, his tail tucked. Ryan could feel the rapid pounding of his heart against his arm. He was terrified.

Good.

The wolf swallowed hard, his voice breaking. "I swear—I didn't know Zack was gonna do *that*!" His voice cracked, eyes welling with tears. "We were just supposed to scare Jamie a little—just to put him in his place, but then—" He sucked in a shaky breath. "Then Zack lost his shit, man! We didn't know he was gonna—gonna beat the hell out of him like that!"

Ryan's stomach twisted with rage. He *wanted* to throw this guy through the glass, wanted to make him feel what Jamie had felt, but instead, he let his voice drop into something even colder.

"You *helped* grab him," Ryan snarled. "You *let* this happen."

The wolf whimpered, squeezing his eyes shut. "I know! I fucking know!" His breath came out in shudders now, his whole body trembling. "I tried to stop it, I swear! I told him it was enough—but he wouldn't listen! He enjoyed it, man! And I—I couldn't stop him."

Ryan's grip tightened.

The wolf sobbed, genuine, pitiful. "I'm done with Zack! He's fucking insane! I was just some idiot trying to be tough—I didn't sign up for *that*!"

Ryan's jaw clenched, his breath ragged, but slowly, his grip eased just slightly. "Where is he?"

The wolf sniffled, blinking rapidly. "He's holed up with some guys over on 8th Avenue Some shitty old house on the south end." He shuddered, shaking his head. "I swear—I'm done with him. I want nothing to do with that psycho."

Ryan studied him, his own breath heavy. He could feel the fear rolling off the guy. He wasn't lying. He was a pathetic, spineless coward, but he wasn't lying.

Slowly, Ryan released his grip, stepping back. The wolf

gasped for air, pressing himself against the door like he still expected Ryan to attack.

Ryan didn't say another word.

He turned and walked away, fists clenched, heart burning with fury.

He had what he needed.

And he was going to find the man who hurt who he loved most.

The rhythmic beeping of Jamie's monitors filled the silent hospital room, a metronome to Ryan's restless thoughts. He sat beside Jamie's bed as he had for the past week, his body hunched over, forearms resting on his knees. His fingers absentmindedly traced circles over Jamie's paw, holding it carefully, protectively.

But his mind wasn't here.

His mind was *there.*

Back in that parking lot. Back to Jamie's body being ripped away from him. Back to the brutal fists and kicks that had left Jamie battered, unconscious, and alone on that pier. Every bruise that painted Jamie's once-soft skin, every bandage wrapped around him, every silent hour that passed where Jamie should've been awake, laughing, teasing him—all of it boiled beneath Ryan's skin like a wildfire.

His free hand slid into his hoodie pocket, fingers brushing over the crumpled paper he had stuffed there before returning to the hospital. The address. *Zack's location.*

Ryan clenched it so tight it nearly tore.

The door creaked open behind him, but Ryan didn't look up. He already knew who it was by the familiar weight of the footsteps.

Sam.

Ryan felt his friend pause at the threshold, his presence warm but cautious. "You're still here," Sam said quietly, his voice careful, deliberate.

Ryan didn't respond.

The silence stretched between them before Sam took another step forward. Ryan sensed it before he saw it—Sam's eyes flicking downward, locking onto the crumpled paper in Ryan's hand.

"...What's that?" Sam asked.

Ryan kept his gaze fixed on Jamie's unmoving face.

Sam moved closer. Ryan heard the soft shuffle of his sneakers against the tile, then the rustle of fabric as Sam crouched beside him, his voice dipping lower. "Ryan."

Ryan swallowed hard, but the tightness in his chest only expanded.

Sam reached out slowly, cautiously, his fingers barely grazing the edge of the paper. And then he read it. The scribbled name. The address.

Sam's face fell.

Ryan still didn't look at him. But he could feel the shift—the sudden, tangible worry in Sam's whole being.

"You found him," Sam murmured, realization dawning in his voice.

Ryan's grip tightened. His nails dug into the paper as his breaths grew heavier.

Sam exhaled, his head dipping slightly, already anticipating the fight before it started. "Ryan...whatever you're thinking, it's not the answer."

Ryan's jaw clenched. "And what *is* the answer, Sam?" His voice was hoarse, barely above a whisper, but laced with something raw.

Sam didn't hesitate. "You stay here. You stay with Jamie. You don't throw yourself into something reckless—"

Ryan let out a bitter, humorless laugh, finally turning to look at him. His eyes were wild, desperate, *angry*. "And what do I do while I stay here, huh? Just sit around? Wait?" his voice cracked. "Wait for what? For justice? For someone else to fix it?" He shook his head. "No, Sam. I can't."

Sam's face softened, but his voice remained firm. "Ryan, listen to me—"

"No, *you* listen to me!" Ryan snapped, sudden tears spilling down his cheeks. His whole body trembled, his breath coming out uneven. "You don't get it, Sam!"

Sam flinched slightly, but Ryan didn't stop.

"You have someone now," Ryan spat, his voice thick with emotion. "You're happy. You moved on. You found something good." His throat bobbed as another tear streaked down his fur. "I lost you."

Sam's eyes widened slightly, but Ryan barely noticed. He was unraveling, raw and exposed.

"And now I found someone," Ryan choked, gripping the bed rail like it was the only thing keeping him upright. His breath hitched violently, his words cracking under the weight of them. "I found Jamie, and now he's been taken from me too!"

The room fell silent except for Ryan's ragged breathing.

Sam looked at him, eyes filled with something deep and unreadable—guilt, sorrow, maybe even love.

Ryan shook his head, wiping at his face roughly before stepping back. "I can't just sit here." His voice was quieter now, but no less certain.

"Ryan, *please*—"

But Ryan was already moving.

He turned and bolted for the door, the paper still crumpled in his fist.

"Ryan!" Sam lunged forward, trying to grab him, but Ryan was already out the door, his injured body running on sheer adrenaline.

Sam pushed through the threshold, but as he reached the hallway—

The elevator doors slid shut, sealing Ryan inside.

Sam's breath caught in his throat, his hands curling into fists as he watched the glowing number above the doors descend.

He slammed a fist against the wall.

"Shit."

The streets were quiet, eerily still as Ryan pulled up to the abandoned house. The headlights of his car cut through the darkness, illuminating the dilapidated structure—boarded-up windows, a sagging porch, the kind of place that had long been forgotten by the city. The air was thick with the stench of damp wood, garbage, and something stale, something *rotten.*

Ryan killed the engine and sat for a moment, gripping the steering wheel tightly. His heart hammered in his chest, his breath slow and controlled, but beneath it all was rage. A fire burning so hot it felt like it might consume him.

Then, movement.

Zack.

The red wolf emerged from the house, his hood pulled up, his posture stiff. He moved quickly, his eyes flicking around warily as he stepped off the porch and headed toward an alley down the block.

Ryan clenched his jaw and slipped out of the car, keeping his steps silent as he moved fast—circling around to the opposite end of the alley. His pulse pounded in his ears, every muscle in his battered body thrumming with adrenaline.

Zack was getting closer.

Ryan's breath came slow, controlled.

Then, just as Zack was about to pass him—

Ryan lunged.

They hit the ground hard, gravel scraping against fur and fabric as they rolled, limbs grappling in the dirt. Zack snarled, trying to throw Ryan off, but Ryan held firm, the sheer force of his fury giving him strength beyond his injuries.

They tumbled, kicking up dust and rocks, fists swinging wildly. Zack landed a hit against Ryan's ribs, sending a sharp jolt of pain through him, but Ryan barely felt it. He shoved Zack back, twisting their bodies until he was on top, pinning the wolf beneath him.

"You son of a bitch!" Ryan roared, grabbing Zack by the collar and slamming him into the dirt. His vision blurred with white-hot fury, every muscle in his body trembling as he raised a fist.

Zack coughed, groaning as he tried to push Ryan off, but Ryan held him down, his breath coming out in ragged, furious bursts.

"You hurt him!" Ryan bellowed, his knuckles tightening, his body coiled and ready to destroy. "You hurt Jamie! Why?!"

Zack flinched, his hands coming up defensively. "I—I—"

Ryan barely heard him. The blood in his veins was molten, his vision swimming with the memory of Jamie's bruised and broken body, his lifeless frame in that hospital bed. He wanted to end this—to make Zack feel every ounce of suffering he had inflicted.

He wound his fist back.

But then—

Jamie's voice.

"*Ryan, stop!*"

It wasn't real. It wasn't here. But it was in his mind.

His body froze.

Ryan's chest heaved, his fist still trembling in the air, but the fire inside of him wavered—just enough for him to see.

Zack wasn't fighting anymore.

The red wolf lay beneath him, breathing hard, his hood fallen back to reveal a swollen black eye, a split lip, bruises scattered across his jaw and neck. His arms were up in surrender, his entire body shaking.

He had already been beaten.

Ryan stared, his breath uneven, the ringing in his ears slowly fading into the sounds of their ragged breathing.

Zack wasn't cocky. He wasn't sneering or taunting. He was frightened.

A slight whimper left his lips as Ryan's grip on his collar tightened.

Ryan's mind screamed at him to finish what he started, to make him pay—but Jamie's voice echoed again in his head.

Jamie wouldn't want this.

Jamie wouldn't want him to become this.

Ryan growled, his frustration and pain twisting together into something almost unbearable. His whole body shook with the effort of restraint as he yanked Zack up by his hoodie, glaring daggers into his bruised and battered face.

"You hurt the person I love," Ryan seethed, his voice low, deadly.

Zack swallowed, his pupils blown wide with fear.

Ryan's breath was shaky, fury still rolling through him, but he didn't move. He just held him there, forcing Zack to see him, to feel every ounce of the rage he had earned.

"Give me one reason," Ryan growled, his claws digging into Zack's shirt, "one *good* reason why I shouldn't make sure you never hurt anyone again."

Zack scowled, his ears twitching in barely restrained frustration as he averted his gaze. His breath was uneven, coming in sharp inhales and shaky exhales, and though he tried to hide it, Ryan could see the slight quiver in his paws, the way his tail hung limply behind him.

There was moisture in Zack's eyes, but he furiously blinked it away, jaw tightening as he struggled to keep his composure. "They—" his voice cracked, and he clenched his teeth before forcing himself to continue. His tail flicked once behind him, erratic and tense. "The people I work with...they saw what happened."

Ryan stayed silent, his own ears still pinned back, his grip iron-tight on Zack's collar.

Zack let out a bitter, humorless laugh, though there was nothing amused about the way his lip curled. His ears pressed flat against his skull as if even admitting it hurt. "They're furious with me," he muttered, tail giving a single, angry flick. "Said my stupidity brought too much attention to them. That now, because of my reckless fucking choice, they have to move locations, scrap everything, start over."

Ryan narrowed his eyes, searching Zack's bruised face for any sign of deception.

"They already kicked the shit out of me for it," Zack admitted, wiping a paw roughly over his snout as if trying to erase the shame along with the blood. His tail curled slightly inward, defensive. "So don't worry, you weren't the first one to get your licks in."

He finally looked back at Ryan, his expression hard, but his body defeated. His ears stayed low, his posture less combative and more...resigned. "I'm getting the fuck out of here," he said simply. "And you won't have trouble from me anymore."

Ryan didn't move at first, his breathing still heavy, tail bristling behind him. Every instinct in his body screamed to keep going, to finish it, to take everything Zack had stolen from Jamie and make him pay.

But then he saw it—Zack wasn't fighting anymore. His ears remained flattened, his tail tucked just slightly, his beaten face not sneering or smug but raw.

Ryan loosened his grip. The hoodie fabric slipped from his fingers as Zack let out a shaky breath, his shoulders sagging slightly.

Ryan straightened up, his golden retriever tail flicking sharply behind him, still bristling with unspent fury. His ears were still back, his body still humming with the need to do more, but he forced himself to step away. "If you *ever* get near my hyena again," he growled, voice dangerously low, "there won't be any mercy."

Zack scoffed, trying to wipe at the dried blood on his lip, though his movements were slow and sluggish. His tail swayed once, lazily, as if he were exhausted even standing upright.

Then—

"Holy shit."

Ryan's ears flicked toward the familiar voice, his body tensing instinctively.

Sam.

Ryan turned his head just in time to see Sam running toward them, his eyes wide, his tail flaring slightly in alarm.

For a moment, Sam just stared at the scene—Ryan, looking like he'd been through hell and back, Zack, beaten and barely standing.

Ryan's breath hitched, his own tail stiffening, the last of the adrenaline still pulsing through him.

Sam's ears twitched in disbelief, his sharp gaze flicking between them before Zack let out a weak, raspy laugh.

"Relax, nurse boy," Zack rasped, spitting to the side. He tried wiping at his fur again, though it barely did anything. "He didn't do this."

Sam's eyes snapped to Ryan in shock, but Zack was already turning away, shaking his head and pulling a cigarette from his pocket. He flicked his lighter, the flame momentarily casting harsh shadows across his face as he took a long drag.

Then, as he exhaled, he turned his head and smirked weakly at Ryan.

Zack exhaled a long stream of smoke, his swollen eyes half-lidded as he watched Ryan crumple onto the curb. His tail gave a lazy flick, his body still tense but clearly exhausted. He took another slow drag before turning on his heel, rolling his shoulders with a wince.

Ryan barely registered the movement, his mind spinning, his heartbeat pounding so loudly in his ears that everything else felt muted.

Zack took a few steps away before pausing, glancing back over his shoulder. His red fur was still matted with blood, and under the dim glow of the streetlights, he looked smaller than before—beaten, tired, finished.

"You really did get yourself a guard dog, Jamie," Zack muttered, the cigarette bobbing between his lips as he gave a half-hearted smirk.

Ryan just stared, his ears twitching slightly, but he didn't respond. His golden retriever tail barely flicked, his body too drained to do anything but exist in the weight of the moment.

Zack huffed, taking one last deep inhale before flicking the cigarette onto the pavement and grinding it out with his boot. With that, he shoved his hands into the pockets of his hoodie and walked away, his tail limp, his steps slow and uneven.

Ryan watched him disappear into the shadows of the alley, the finality of it settling heavily in his chest.

A long, shaky breath left his lips, and the moment Zack was gone, the adrenaline that had been fueling him completely abandoned him. His muscles ached, his limbs trembled, and his skull still throbbed from his previous injuries. The fight, the chase, the *rage*—all of it drained out of him, leaving him feeling hollow.

He barely felt Sam's presence until the weight of a paw landed gently on his shoulder.

"Ryan," Sam said again, softer now, the concern evident in his voice.

Ryan's ears flicked slightly, but he didn't look up. His breathing was unsteady, his tail twitching weakly against the pavement.

Sam shifted slightly beside him, his tail flicking once as he took in the sheer exhaustion written all over Ryan's frame.

"I'm sorry—"

Ryan shook his head, exhaling shakily before cutting him off.

"What I said wasn't fair," he murmured, voice hoarse, heavy with emotion. His fingers twitched against his knees, his ears still pinned back. "I—I *am* happy for you, Sam. I really am." His throat bobbed, his vision still blurry with exhaustion. "It was jealousy. And fear. And I shouldn't have said those things."

Sam let out a small breath, watching Ryan closely before his paw gave a gentle squeeze on his shoulder, his tail giving the faintest flick of reassurance.

"Yeah," Sam said softly. "But I get it."

Ryan finally turned to look at him, his eyes rimmed with exhaustion, the weight of the night pressing into every fiber of his being. Sam's expression was steady, warm, and knowing.

And somehow, after everything, that was enough.

The two of them sat in silence for a long moment, the quiet night stretching around them. Ryan's body felt heavy, like the weight of everything had finally caught up to him all at once. His ears drooped slightly, his tail resting motionless against the curb. Sam stayed beside him, unmoving, his presence steady and grounding.

The cold pavement pressed into Ryan's palms, his breath still shaky but no longer ragged with anger. The fire that had consumed him just minutes ago had simmered into something else—something quieter, but no less painful.

Sam shifted beside him, his tail flicking once as if debating something. Then, he exhaled and turned to Ryan.

"There's something you need to know," he said gently, watching Ryan carefully.

Ryan finally looked at him, his ears perking up slightly at the shift in Sam's tone.

Sam gave him a small, hesitant nod before continuing. "Jamie's waking up."

Ryan's body stiffened. His breath hitched.

"He's still groggy," Sam went on, his voice measured but steady, "not totally aware, but the doctors think he'll be coming to soon."

Ryan stared, his brain struggling to process the words.

Jamie. *Waking up.*

The exhaustion that had been weighing him down evaporated in an instant. He moved, pushing himself up so fast that his battered ribs screamed in protest, but he barely felt it. His tail flicked sharply behind him, his ears standing tall as his mind raced.

"I need to be there," he said, voice firm and determined.

Sam didn't argue. He just stood up beside him, giving a small nod. "Let's go."

Without another word, the two of them rushed toward the car, the night stretching long behind them, but Ryan's mind was already elsewhere.

Back in that hospital room.

Back to Jamie.

Chapter 12

RYAN turned the corner, his breath caught in his throat, his heartbeat thundering in his ears.

And then he saw him.

Jamie.

His eyes were open, golden and hazy with exhaustion but alive. He was sitting upright in bed, his wrist still wrapped in a cast, his body marked with bruises, but he was there. Awake. He was politely nodding as the nurse took his vitals, his expression unreadable but composed in that quiet way that was so uniquely *him.*

Ryan's whole body froze.

Then, something inside him shattered.

Tears welled in his eyes so fast he barely registered them spilling down his cheeks. His legs felt weak, his chest tight with so much overwhelming emotion that he could hardly breathe. His vision blurred as he took a shaky step forward, his entire world narrowing down to the boy in front of him.

As Jamie glanced up, his gaze landed on Ryan.

His expression flickered—first with surprise, then with something deeper. His ears twitched, his tail curling slightly at his side as his lips parted, blinking rapidly as if trying to ground himself.

For a brief moment, his eyes softened into something warm, something almost relieved—but then guilt crept in. Pain. His fingers tightened on the hospital blanket, his throat bobbing as he quickly blinked away the moisture in his eyes. Jamie wasn't someone who showed emotion easily, but it was there, just beneath the surface.

Ryan reached the doorway just as the nurse finished up, giving him a knowing look before excusing herself. Sam lingered in the hall, his face damp with tears but smiling, choosing to stay back and give them space.

Ryan didn't move, didn't speak.

He just stood there, staring at Jamie like he had seen a ghost, because in some ways, he had.

Jamie met his gaze, his own eyes glistening, but it was Jamie who moved first.

Before Ryan could blink, Jamie was standing, his movements careful but steady. He took a slow step forward, and then another, until he was right in front of Ryan, looking up at him with tired but steady golden eyes.

His paws lifted, landing on Ryan's cheeks, warm and gentle.

And then he smiled.

"I'm here," Jamie murmured, his voice quiet but sure. "And I'm not going anywhere."

A sob broke from Ryan's throat before he could stop it.

He lunged, wrapping his arms around Jamie in a desperate, almost crushing embrace. Jamie let out a soft *oof*, startled, but after a split second, he melted into Ryan's hold, his arms looping around Ryan's back, his head tucking under Ryan's chin.

Ryan clutched him tightly, pressing Jamie against him as if he could somehow shield him from ever being hurt again. His paws splayed over Jamie's back, feeling the warmth of his body, the way his fur felt soft against his own. His heartbeat pounded in his ears, but it was drowned out by the steady, real presence of Jamie in his arms.

Jamie smelled like the faint hospital scent of antiseptic, but underneath it was *him*—the familiar, natural scent that Ryan had come to crave. His weight, the way his chest rose and fell against Ryan's, the way his paws gripped the fabric of Ryan's hoodie, *everything* was real.

He was alive.

"I can't believe I almost lost you," Ryan choked, his voice muffled against Jamie's shoulder. His whole body trembled as he held him closer. "I'm so sorry. I wasn't strong enough."

Jamie exhaled slowly, and then he gently pulled back, just enough to meet Ryan's gaze.

His expression was serious, firm, but his touch was gentle as he cupped Ryan's cheek again, his thumb brushing lightly against the fur damp with tears.

"You did nothing wrong, Ryan," he said, voice steadier now. "You did everything you could." His ears flicked slightly, his eyes searching Ryan's. "When I saw you lying there, I thought the worst. I thought—I thought I was losing you." His throat bobbed, his tail curling slightly behind him. "I fought. I fought as hard as I could until I wasn't able to move anymore. And I know you did the same."

Jamie's gaze didn't waver, even as his voice softened into something more vulnerable. "We both did all we could," he murmured. "And I'm just glad I have you here with me now."

Ryan stared at him, his vision still blurred, his heart still aching—but in a different way now.

Jamie was right.

They had fought. They had survived.

Ryan swallowed hard, sniffling as another tear rolled down his cheek. But this time, he smiled.

A quiet, trembling, relieved smile.

Jamie's ears flicked at the sight of it, his own lips twitching upward in response.

Ryan let out a breathy laugh, still sniffling as he leaned into Jamie's touch, nuzzling against his palm slightly before murmuring, "You're really bad at resting, you know that?"

Jamie huffed, amused. "You're one to talk."

Ryan chuckled softly, his tail swaying behind him.

For the first time in what felt like forever, the weight pressing down on his chest lifted.

Ryan barely had a second to react before Jamie leaned in, closing the space between them and pressing his lips against Ryan's.

Ryan's ears shot up in surprise, his tail giving a single, stunned flick. Jamie had always been shy about initiating things, but here he was, kissing him first.

The shock melted away in an instant.

Ryan exhaled softly through his nose, his hands instinctively cupping Jamie's waist as he leaned into the kiss. Jamie's lips were warm, soft, his touch firm but hesitant, like he was still testing his own confidence. Ryan's tail swayed behind him as he deepened the kiss slightly, savoring the moment, the feeling of Jamie alive and safe in his arms.

When they finally broke apart, Jamie let out a small, quiet chuckle, his muzzle still close enough that Ryan could feel his breath.

"Now," Jamie murmured, smirking slightly, "can you stop being so sad, you big sap?"

Ryan let out a breathy laugh, his ears folding back slightly in embarrassment as he rubbed the back of his head. "No promises," he admitted, his goofy grin widening as Jamie rolled his eyes at him.

With a small huff, Jamie pointed toward the hospital bed. "Alright, muscles, if you're done crying over me, *I* would like to sit down now."

Ryan grinned but obeyed, gently guiding Jamie back onto

the bed with exaggerated care. Jamie gave him a look but didn't protest as he settled in.

The next morning, sunlight filtered in through the hospital windows, casting a soft glow over the room.

Ryan was sitting in the chair beside Jamie's bed, his chin resting in his palm, watching as the nurse gave him the final once-over for discharge.

Jamie stretched his free arm, sighing in relief as his freshly wrapped wrist—now secured in a splint instead of a cast—felt far less restrictive. "So I'm finally free?" he asked, his ears twitching hopefully.

The nurse chuckled. "You're free. But *gentle* movements with that wrist. No sudden impacts, no heavy lifting."

Jamie made a vague *yeah, yeah* motion with his good paw before turning to Ryan. "Guess you'll have to open all my jars for me now," he teased.

Ryan smirked. "So, what I'm hearing is, I have *another* reason to flex on you."

Jamie scoffed but couldn't help the small smile pulling at his lips.

As they made their way out of the hospital, Ryan pulled out his phone and shot off a text to their group chat.

Ryan: *Jamie's finally getting out of here.*

The responses came almost immediately.

Bandaid: "*THANK THE LORD THE PRINCE LIVES!*"

Lysander: "*That is excellent news. Please let us know if you need anything.*"

Sam: "*Tell him we're all waiting to see him when he's ready.*"

Ryan smiled down at his phone before glancing at Jamie, who was busy adjusting his hoodie sleeve over his splint.

"You ready to get the hell out of here?" Ryan asked, nudging him gently.

Jamie shot him a *duh* look. "If I never see this place again, it'll be too soon."

Ryan chuckled as they stepped outside, the cool breeze ruffling their fur. He knew Jamie was putting up a strong front, but he also knew Jamie needed rest.

So, when they got back to Jamie's place, Ryan didn't let him do anything.

He helped him get comfortable, made sure he ate something, and—despite Jamie's stubborn insistence that he was fine—refused to leave.

And at some point, as the day faded into evening, they found themselves on the couch.

Jamie curled into Ryan's chest, his body finally giving into the exhaustion that had been creeping up on him. His breath was slow and steady, his injured paw resting carefully against Ryan's ribs.

Ryan held him tight, one arm draped protectively over Jamie's side, his nose nestled into the hyena's soft fur. His tail curled loosely behind them, but his grip on Jamie was firm—like his body refused to let go, like some part of him still feared Jamie might disappear.

Jamie shifted slightly in his sleep, nuzzling in closer with a small, content sigh.

Ryan pressed a lingering kiss against the top of his head, his own eyes growing heavy.

For the first time in weeks, Ryan finally allowed himself to relax.

Jamie was safe. He was still here.

And Ryan wasn't letting him go.

The morning light filtered through the curtains, casting a warm glow over the couch where Ryan and Jamie still lay tangled together. Ryan stirred first, blinking slowly as he registered the soft weight pressed against his chest—Jamie, still curled into him, his breath slow and even.

Ryan's tail flicked once, a soft smile tugging at his lips. He lifted a paw, brushing a few stray strands of Jamie's brown hair from his face before leaning down and pressing a gentle kiss to his forehead.

Jamie murmured something incoherent, shifting slightly, his eyes fluttering open.

Ryan grinned. "Good morning, sleeping beauty."

Jamie groaned, nuzzling further into Ryan's chest. "Too early," he muttered, his voice still thick with sleep.

Ryan chuckled, placing another soft kiss on Jamie's temple. "I'll go get us some breakfast," he said, carefully untangling himself and stretching.

Jamie blinked up at him sleepily, rubbing at his eyes with his uninjured paw. "Mm...make it good."

Ryan smirked. "Only the best for you, *your highness*."

Jamie huffed, but there was a tiny, pleased smile on his lips as he sunk back into the couch.

Ryan quickly made them a simple breakfast—some toast, eggs, and fruit—making sure Jamie ate before giving him a gentle nuzzle.

"I gotta go pick up Max before Bandaid completely turns him into a little menace," Ryan said with a teasing smirk.

Jamie stretched, his tail flicking lazily. "Good luck. That rabbit's got a lot of energy from what you've told me."

Ryan laughed, kissing Jamie's forehead one last time before grabbing his keys and heading out.

As soon as Ryan opened the door to Bandaid's place, he was ambushed.

"RYAN!"

Bandaid launched himself at him, wrapping his arms around Ryan in a tight, warm hug, his smaller but surprisingly strong frame squeezing the air out of Ryan's lungs.

Ryan let out a breathy laugh, hugging him back.

"I'm so happy Jamie's okay," Bandaid said, his voice thick with emotion. His usual playful tone was still there, but there was something genuine behind it. "And I'm so relieved you're okay too."

Ryan's ears flicked, warmth settling in his chest.

Bandaid pulled back slightly, his pink-bandaid-covered paws gripping Ryan's shoulders. "Dude, you've been through hell. The last few weeks have been nothing but torture, and yet you *still* kept going. That's...that's brave as hell, Ryan." His expression softened, sincerity in his big, round eyes. "Me, Lys, Sam—we're always here for you. No matter what."

Ryan swallowed the lump in his throat, his tail flicking behind him. "Thanks, Bandaid," he murmured, giving his friend's arm a squeeze. "That means a lot."

Bandaid grinned and, true to himself, immediately lightened the mood. "Okay, enough sap. Go get your dumb dog before he eats all my protein bars."

Ryan snorted as he turned toward the couch. "Max, come here, buddy!"

The golden-coated dog perked up at the sound of his name before bounding toward Ryan, tail wagging furiously. Ryan crouched down, letting Max shove his face into his chest, licking at his muzzle and whimpering with excitement.

Ryan laughed, running his paws through Max's thick fur and nuzzling against him. "I missed you too, bud," he murmured, pressing his forehead against Max's. His tail swayed softly behind him. "Jamie's okay. We're gonna be okay."

Max let out a happy huff, licking Ryan's face again before wiggling happily.

Ryan grinned, giving him one last pat before standing. "Alright, we're heading home."

Bandaid waved dramatically. "Tell Jamie he owes me a 'thank you' for keeping his big buff boyfriend sane."

Ryan rolled his eyes with a smirk. "I'll let him know."

As Ryan stepped into his apartment, Max trotted in beside him, immediately hopping onto his dog bed with a satisfied thump. Ryan chuckled and moved to empty his pockets onto the counter when—

Knock knock.

Ryan's ears twitched. He wasn't expecting anyone.

He walked over, unlocking the door, and when it swung open—

As Ryan opened the door, he froze for a moment. Standing on the other side was Chloe.

She looked different—smaller, somehow. Her ears were slightly folded back, her arms crossed over her stomach, and there was an unmistakable uncertainty in her posture. The usual sharpness in her eyes was gone, replaced with something softer.

"Hey," she said quietly, shifting on her feet. "Can I...can I come in?"

Ryan hesitated for only a second before stepping aside. "Yeah, of course."

She stepped inside, glancing around as she took in the space. "It looks nice," she commented, her voice measured but genuine.

Ryan gave a small smile, rubbing the back of his head. "Yeah, I've been keeping busy."

Chloe nodded, then let out a slow breath. When she turned to face him, her expression was conflicted—like she was searching for the right words.

"I, um..." She sighed, her ears folding down further. "I saw what happened on the news."

Ryan stiffened slightly but said nothing, waiting.

Chloe's tail flicked anxiously behind her, and for the first time since she walked in, she looked ashamed. "I—I was worried about you," she admitted. "But more than that, I...I realized something." She swallowed, her gaze lowering. "When we were together, I made things so much worse for you. And I didn't see it at the time, but I see it now."

Ryan tilted his head slightly, his chest tightening at the sudden vulnerability in her voice.

She sniffed, shaking her head at herself. "It must've been so hard for you," she continued, voice thick with guilt. "Being gay. Hiding it. Feeling like you had to fit into something that wasn't you, and—and I added to that. I made you feel trapped, like you had to prove something, and I wasn't what you needed." Her fingers clenched the hem of her sleeve. "I look back on it now, and I realize how much I hurt you by ignoring what was right in front of me."

Ryan's breath hitched slightly.

He'd spent years feeling guilt about their relationship—about leading her on, about not being able to be what she deserved. But hearing *this* from *her*...

It was like a weight he hadn't realized he was carrying had been lifted.

Chloe exhaled shakily before meeting his gaze. "I just...I want you to know that I get it now. I get why it happened the way it did. And I'm so sorry that I didn't make it easier for you."

Ryan blinked, his ears twitching slightly in surprise.

"I was selfish," she admitted, her voice quieter now. "I cared more about what I wanted than about what *you* needed. And I can't change the past, but I just..." She let out a slow breath. "I wanted to say it. I needed to say it."

Ryan's throat tightened, but he managed a small, grateful smile. "Thank you," he murmured. "That...that really means a lot."

They stood there in comfortable silence for a moment, a quiet understanding settling between them.

After a beat, Chloe cleared her throat, offering a small smile. "I, uh...I'm seeing someone now," she said, shifting on her feet. "And I really like him."

Ryan's ears perked slightly, his tail giving a faint flick. "Yeah?" He grinned. "That's great, Chloe. I'm happy for you."

She studied him for a moment, then tilted her head. "And you?"

Ryan felt warmth bloom in his chest. His tail swayed behind him as his thoughts immediately drifted to Jamie.

"I met someone," he admitted, voice soft.

Chloe's lips parted slightly before a knowing smile tugged at the corners. "You love him," she observed.

Ryan huffed a laugh, ears flicking back slightly as his face heated up. "Yeah," he murmured. "I do."

Time passed as they caught up, exchanging stories about their lives, filling in the gaps of time they had lost.

Eventually, Chloe sighed, glancing at the door. "I should go."

Ryan walked her over, but before she stepped out, she paused, looking at him with something unreadable in her expression.

Then, gently, she reached for his hand.

Her fingers curled around his, her grip warm but light.

Ryan's ears flicked as she squeezed his hand, her gaze soft.

"I'm sorry," she whispered, her voice barely above a breath. "For everything."

Ryan swallowed, his tail stilling behind him.

She hesitated, then let out a quiet laugh. "I hope you're happy, Ryan," she murmured, squeezing his fingers one last time. Then, after a pause, she added, "And I hope Jamie is too."

Ryan felt a wave of emotion swell in his chest—unexpected, but welcomed.

"Thanks, Chloe," he said, offering a small, genuine smile.

She leaned up, pressing a soft, fleeting kiss to his cheek before stepping back. With one last nod, she turned and walked away.

Ryan let out a deep breath as he closed the door, his heart lighter than it had been in years.

Then, his phone buzzed.

Jamie had sent a GIF of a cat peeking through blinds.

Ryan let out a breathy laugh, shaking his head as warmth spread through his chest while texting in response, "Miss me already?"

As the next message came in, Ryan smiled, a sense of peace settling over him.

For the first time in a long, long time—everything felt *right.*

CHAPTER 13

THE next few weeks fell into an easy, comforting rhythm. Jamie was at Ryan's place *constantly*—sometimes for full days, sometimes just stopping by between errands, but most nights ended the same: the two of them curled up together, wrapped in each other's warmth. Jamie's smaller frame fit perfectly against Ryan's, their tails lazily draped over one another as they drifted off to sleep.

At first, Ryan had always told Jamie, "You don't have to stay if you don't want to."

But Jamie never hesitated. "I want to," he would say simply, pressing his face against Ryan's chest.

Ryan had never slept so soundly.

As their bodies healed, they got back into their usual routines. Ryan returned to the gym, and much to everyone's surprise, Jamie started tagging along.

Lysander and Bandaid were *thrilled.*

"Ah, *finally* the hyena joins us in our temple of gains," Bandaid teased one afternoon as they all stood by the lockers.

Jamie rolled his eyes, adjusting the strings of his hoodie. "I just don't want to wither away while Ryan gets stronger than me."

Ryan grinned, giving Jamie's waist a playful squeeze. "Babe, I could already carry you *and* Bandaid at the same time."

Jamie's ears twitched, and his nose scrunched in that way Ryan loved. "Shut up."

But despite his words, Jamie didn't hate the gym. He never lifted like the rest of them, but he enjoyed the routine, the banter, and—though he'd never admit it—the way Ryan would show off for him, tail wagging every time Jamie gave him a lingering glance.

The only thing Jamie couldn't handle?

The showers.

The first time Ryan, Bandaid, and Lysander all peeled off their gym clothes to rinse off, Jamie froze.

His entire face turned *scarlet*. His ears flattened against his head, his tail tucking slightly as he sputtered, "I—um—I can wait outside."

Bandaid, of course, immediately flexed. "Aw, c'mon, Jamie, you don't wanna see the goods?"

Ryan rolled his eyes. "Leave him alone, man."

Jamie, still bright red, turned on his heel and bolted from the locker room.

Ryan laughed as Bandaid smirked. "Oh, that boy is down bad for you."

Lysander sighed, adjusting his towel over his shoulder. "Must you antagonize *everyone*, Bandaid?"

Bandaid simply flexed his legs dramatically. "I am a gift, Lys. My power must be shared."

Ryan just chuckled, shaking his head, but his mind lingered on Jamie—his blushing face, his nervous little twitch of his ears.

Outside the gym, things between them had started to shift.

Most nights, they got...*handsy*.

Ryan would pull Jamie into his lap on the couch, kissing him slow and deep, his paws tracing up his back, over his sides, down his thighs. Jamie would melt against him, tilting his head to give Ryan more access, fingers curling in his fur, their breaths turning heavier.

But every time things got too heated—hands slipping under shirts, hips pressing a little too firmly—they would pause.

Jamie would stiffen slightly, or Ryan would hesitate, both of them *worried*—worried they were pushing too much, moving too fast.

And so, they would stop.

And Ryan was okay with that.

Because *this*—this slow, careful exploration, this building tension, this trust—meant *everything*.

Then came the night everything changed.

They had gone out to dinner, nothing particularly special—just a casual meal at their favorite burger joint. But something about it felt *different* to Ryan. Maybe it was the way Jamie kept catching his eye over the table, that small, knowing smile playing at his lips. Maybe it was the way their knees brushed under the booth, neither of them pulling away.

Or maybe it was the fact that, sitting across from Jamie, watching him laugh softly at something he said, Ryan realized something:

He *wanted* Jamie.

Not just in the teasing, casual way he had thought before. Not just in the playful way they made out on the couch.

He wanted to *be with him*. Fully. Completely.

He wanted to take that next step *together*.

And so, as Jamie finished his last few fries and wiped his paws on his napkin, Ryan made the decision.

Tonight, he was going to make love to Jamie.

The door shut softly behind them, leaving the two of them standing in the quiet, dimly lit space. Jamie hovered near the doorway, shifting on his feet as he took in Ryan's cozy, lived-in apartment. The faint scent of fresh laundry and something faintly woodsy—Ryan's cologne—hung in the air.

Ryan, noticing Jamie's hesitation, set his gym bag down with a casual thud and gave him a reassuring smile. "Hey," he said, stepping closer and sliding an arm around Jamie's waist. "You're good. It's just me, remember?"

Ryan's tail wagged as he pulled Jamie gently toward the couch. "You say that, but you're still here," he teased, dropping onto the cushions and patting his lap.

"C'mere," Ryan teased.

Jamie hesitated for only a second before sitting down, letting Ryan guide him into his arms. The taller hyena-retriever wrapped Jamie up easily, his broad chest warm and solid beneath Jamie's cheek. Ryan's hand slid up and down his back in slow, comforting strokes, and Jamie sighed, his shoulders finally relaxing.

"This isn't so bad, right?" Ryan murmured, his voice soft as he rested his chin on Jamie's head.

Jamie let out a quiet laugh, his hands curling into the fabric of Ryan's shirt. "No. It's nice."

"Nice?" Ryan teased, nudging Jamie's temple with his nose. "Just 'nice'? I'll have you know, I'm a world-class cuddler."

Jamie smirked, his face hidden against Ryan's chest. "Oh yeah? I didn't realize that was a title. But you always seem to know what you're doing."

Ryan chuckled, his hand drifting up to tangle gently in Jamie's hair. "You'd be surprised. But seriously…I'm glad you're here. That uh, we are here"

Jamie looked up at him, his golden-brown eyes catching the softer glow of Ryan's. "Me too," he said quietly, his cheeks tinting pink.

Their faces were close now, the teasing edge giving way to something deeper, more uncertain. Ryan's gaze flicked down to Jamie's lips, and when Jamie didn't pull back, he leaned in, capturing them in a kiss.

It was tentative at first, a gentle press of mouths as they found their rhythm. But as Jamie's hands slid up to Ryan's chest, clutching at the soft fabric of his shirt, Ryan deepened the kiss, his tongue flicking out to taste the edge of Jamie's lips.

Jamie gasped softly, parting his lips to let Ryan in, his breath hitching as the kiss grew more heated. Ryan's hands slipped under the hem of Jamie's hoodie, his fingers warm against the soft fur of his waist.

"Is this okay?" Ryan murmured, his voice husky as he pulled back just enough to search Jamie's face.

Jamie nodded quickly, his ears twitching. "Yeah. It's...really okay."

Ryan smiled, brushing his thumb along Jamie's cheek before leaning in again. He kissed him slower this time, savoring every little sound Jamie made, every hesitant movement of his hands. But soon, Jamie was the one to pull back, his face flushed as he slid off Ryan's lap and knelt between his knees.

Ryan blinked, his tail flicking against the couch as he looked down at Jamie. "What are you doing?"

Jamie's cheeks were burning, but his eyes were steady as he rested his hands on Ryan's thighs. "I...I want to do this," he said softly.

Ryan's breath caught in his throat. "Jamie, you don't have to—"

"I know," Jamie interrupted, his voice firmer now. "I want to. You've been so patient with me, and...I want to do something for you."

Ryan's heart squeezed at the vulnerability in Jamie's voice. His plans had taken an unexpected turn, a welcomed one. He reached down, his hand gently cupping Jamie's cheek. "Okay," he said, his voice thick. "But we take this slow. You set the pace."

Jamie nodded, his hands sliding up to the waistband of Ryan's joggers. He hesitated for just a moment, looking up at Ryan, who gave him a reassuring nod.

Slowly, Jamie tugged the fabric down, revealing the golden-tan fur of Ryan's thighs and the hardened length between them.

Jamie bit his lip, his cheeks flushing deeper as he wrapped his fingers tentatively around Ryan's cock. Ryan let out a soft groan, his hips shifting slightly at the touch.

"Take your time," Ryan murmured, his voice low and encouraging. His hand came to rest on Jamie's head, his fingers threading gently through the soft fur there.

Jamie's lips parted as he leaned closer, his breath warm against Ryan's skin. His first touch was hesitant—a soft, uncertain brush of his tongue against the tip—but the way Ryan's breath hitched made his confidence grow. He pressed forward, wrapping his lips around the head as his hand began to stroke the base.

"Fuck, Jamie..." Ryan breathed, his head falling back against the couch. His thighs tensed under Jamie's hands, and his tail thumped lazily against the cushions.

Encouraged by the sounds Ryan made, Jamie moved a little deeper, his tongue tracing along the underside as his hand followed the rhythm of his mouth. Ryan's breathing grew heavier, his fingers tightening slightly in Jamie's hair.

"You're doing so good," Ryan murmured, his voice rough and full of affection. "God, you're perfect..."

Jamie hummed softly, the vibration drawing another groan

from Ryan. He looked up through his lashes, catching the way Ryan's eyes were half-lidded with pleasure, his expression both tender and utterly undone.

The connection between them was electric, the air thick with warmth and trust. Jamie's movements grew bolder as he found his rhythm, and Ryan's breathing became more ragged, his body taut with tension.

"Jamie—" Ryan's voice broke, his hand gently tugging Jamie back. Jamie released him with a soft pop, looking up in confusion.

"Did I mess up?" Jamie asked, his voice small.

Ryan shook his head quickly, pulling Jamie up into his lap. "No. You were perfect," he said, his voice thick with emotion. "I just...I didn't want to finish without taking care of you, too."

Jamie blinked, his cheeks pink as Ryan kissed him deeply. "You're not getting out of this that easily," Ryan murmured against his lips, his hands sliding down Jamie's back.

Ryan's lips trailed down Jamie's neck, warm and teasing as he pulled him back into his lap. Jamie's breath hitched, his hands curling into the fabric of Ryan's shirt as the larger man kissed him deeply.

"R-Ryan," Jamie stammered between kisses, his voice trembling with both excitement and nervousness.

Ryan pulled back just enough to meet Jamie's eyes, his expression soft but burning with desire. "You good?" he asked, his voice husky as his hands traced slow circles along Jamie's lower back.

Jamie nodded quickly, though his ears twitched with nerves. "Yeah, I just...I don't know what to do."

Ryan smiled, pressing a gentle kiss to Jamie's forehead. "You don't have to do anything," he murmured, his voice low and reassuring. "Just let me take care of you."

Jamie's heart skipped at the promise in Ryan's words, and he let himself relax as Ryan's hands slid lower, gripping his hips firmly. With a gentle nudge, Ryan guided him to stand, his golden eyes glinting as he looked up at Jamie.

"Turn around for me," Ryan said softly, his voice like velvet.

Jamie hesitated, his cheeks burning, but the way Ryan's hands squeezed his hips gently gave him the courage to move. He turned slowly, his back to Ryan, and felt those warm hands trail up his sides before settling on the waistband of his jeans.

"Can I?" Ryan asked, his voice warm and patient as his thumbs hooked into the fabric.

Jamie swallowed hard, nodding. "Yeah," he said, his voice barely above a whisper.

Ryan didn't rush, pulling Jamie's jeans down inch by inch, the movement deliberate and reverent. Jamie's tail flicked nervously as the cool air hit his skin, but Ryan's hands were there, soothing and steady, sliding along his thighs.

"Jamie," Ryan murmured, his voice filled with awe as his hands moved to grip Jamie's hips. "You're gorgeous."

Jamie's ears flattened, his face burning as he glanced over his shoulder. "You're just saying that."

Ryan laughed softly, leaning forward to press a kiss to the small of Jamie's back. "I don't just say things I don't mean," he said, his breath warm against Jamie's skin. "Now, let me show you."

Jamie shivered as Ryan guided him to kneel on the couch, his hands bracing against the cushions. Ryan shifted behind him, his warm palms spreading over Jamie's hips and gently urging him to arch.

"Ryan, I—" Jamie started, but his words cut off in a gasp as Ryan's hands slid down, his thumbs brushing along the sensitive curve of Jamie's backside.

"Trust me," Ryan murmured, his voice low and soothing as he kissed the base of Jamie's spine.

Jamie's tail twitched, but he didn't pull away, his breath

catching as Ryan's lips trailed lower. The first flick of Ryan's tongue made Jamie's whole body tense, a sharp gasp escaping him as Ryan's grip on his hips tightened.

"Relax," Ryan murmured, his voice vibrating against Jamie's skin. "I've got you."

Jamie exhaled shakily, his fingers gripping the cushions as Ryan's tongue began to explore, slow and deliberate. The sensation was overwhelming—warm and slick, sending sparks racing up Jamie's spine as Ryan's hands kneaded the soft flesh of his hips.

"Oh my god," Jamie whispered, his voice breathless as Ryan's tongue moved in firm, rhythmic strokes.

Ryan hummed in response, the vibration sending a shiver through Jamie's entire body. He shifted slightly, spreading Jamie open further to give himself better access, his movements both confident and careful.

Jamie's head dropped forward, his breath coming in ragged pants as he tried to process the flood of sensations. Ryan's mouth was relentless, alternating between teasing flicks and deep, purposeful strokes that left Jamie trembling.

"Ryan...I—" Jamie gasped, his voice breaking as one of Ryan's hands slid down to wrap around his thigh, steadying him.

"You're doing so good," Ryan murmured against him, his voice muffled but full of affection. "You taste so good, Jamie. Just let go for me."

Jamie whimpered, his fingers clutching the cushions as his body obeyed, melting into Ryan's touch.

Every flick of Ryan's tongue sent waves of heat coursing through him, his tail twitching helplessly as Ryan worked him over with practiced precision.

The sounds filling the room—Jamie's breathless moans, the wet, intimate noises of Ryan's mouth—only heightened the intensity of the moment. Jamie's legs began to tremble, and he could feel the heat building low in his belly, coiling tighter with every movement of Ryan's tongue.

"Ryan," he gasped, his voice high and strained. "I—Oh god—"

Ryan pulled back just enough to press a kiss to Jamie's trembling thigh, his voice warm and rough as he said, "I've got you. Let it happen babe."

The air between them was thick with heat, their bodies damp with sweat and the lingering traces of Ryan's tongue against Jamie's skin. Jamie trembled, still bent over the arm of the couch, his breath uneven as he turned his head slightly, eyes full of need.

"Ryan...I want you," he whispered, his voice laced with shyness but unmistakable desire.

Ryan swallowed hard. He was new to this, new to the feel of another man's body in this way, but the sight of Jamie—flushed, slick, and waiting—sent a surge of raw hunger through him. He ran his hands down Jamie's back, feeling the way he shuddered under his touch, his muscles tense yet pliant.

The scent of them filled the air—Jamie's warm musk, the salt of sweat, the remnants of cologne mixing with the slick sweetness of Ryan's saliva. It was intoxicating. Ryan leaned in, pressing his chest against Jamie's back, inhaling deeply as he kissed the back of his neck, feeling the heat radiate between them.

"Are you sure?" Ryan murmured, his lips brushing against Jamie's ear.

Jamie nodded, his body pushing back slightly, urging Ryan forward. Ryan's fingers traced along Jamie's hip before gripping him firmly, steadying himself as he eased in. A groan tore from Jamie's throat, his fingers clenching against the couch as he adjusted.

Ryan gasped, the tight, searing heat making his nerves spark. He held still, trying to collect himself, but the way Jamie pulsed around him, the way he let out those breathy, needy whimpers, made restraint nearly impossible. He started to move—slowly at first, reveling in every sensation, every squeeze, every desperate sound Jamie made beneath him.

The couch creaked with their rhythm, their bodies slick against each other as sweat dripped from Ryan's brow onto Jamie's back. He couldn't get enough of the way Jamie smelled, the way his skin felt beneath his hands. He ran his fingers up Jamie's stomach, pressing his palm against the rapid rise and fall of his breath.

"God, you feel so good," Ryan groaned, his voice strained, his control slipping.

Jamie moaned, pushing back harder, his body seeking more. The room filled with the raw sounds of their pleasure, of skin meeting skin, of gasps and murmured curses. The tension coiled tighter, every thrust bringing them closer until Ryan felt Jamie shudder violently beneath him, a cry of ecstasy spilling from his lips as he came, his body clenching around Ryan and pushing him over the edge.

Ryan's release was sudden, overwhelming, his body locking up as waves of pleasure crashed through him. He collapsed forward, his chest slick against Jamie's sweat-damp back, both of them panting, trembling messes. His forehead rested against Jamie's shoulder, his breath warm against his skin as they came down together, bodies still intertwined, spent but sated.

For a moment, neither of them moved, the only sound in the room their ragged breathing and the faint creak of the couch beneath them. Then Ryan pressed a lazy kiss to Jamie's shoulder, a small, satisfied chuckle escaping his lips.

"Well," Ryan panted, still catching his breath, "I think I could get used to this."

Jamie laughed softly, reaching back to squeeze Ryan's thigh. "Yeah," he murmured, his voice husky and blissed out. "Me too."

The air was still thick with warmth, the scent of them lingering in the room as Ryan lay beside Jamie, his chest rising and falling in time with his deep, steady breaths. His body felt heavy in the best way—spent, satisfied, *whole.*

But his mind?

His mind was lost in *Jamie.*

Ryan's blue eyes roamed over the striped hyena beside him, taking in *everything*—the way Jamie's chest still moved slightly faster than normal, the faint flush still lingering beneath his fur, the way his hair had become even more unruly from their time together. His scent was intoxicating, home, something uniquely *him.*

And his eyes—They were sparkling.

Golden, deep, holding a quiet intensity even now, reflecting the dim light of the room. They held a softness Ryan had never seen before, something bare and unguarded.

Ryan swallowed, his tail giving a slow, lazy flick as he reached out, his fingers tracing lightly down Jamie's arm.

Jamie caught him staring.

His ears twitched, his blush darkening, and with a small, almost flustered huff, he glanced away—only to peek back up through his lashes. A moment later, he leaned in, closing the space between them and pressing the softest, most fleeting kiss against Ryan's nose.

Ryan blinked, the trance breaking as warmth spread through his chest.

Jamie smirked slightly at his reaction. "You were staring."

Ryan let out a soft chuckle, his fingers still absentmindedly tracing Jamie's fur. "Can you blame me?" His voice was barely above a whisper, raw with emotion. "You're beautiful."

Jamie's ears pinned slightly, his tail curling as he let out a quiet scoff—but the way he blushed gave him away.

Ryan kept staring, completely enraptured.

This was *his* Jamie—the same Jamie who had shyly helped him hang flyers about a lost dog, the same Jamie who blushed at gym showers and peeked through blinds in silly GIFs, the same Jamie who had fought with everything he had against people who had tried to take everything from them.

They had been through *so much* together.

And now, they were here.

Something inside Ryan's chest ached, something deep and profound and terrifying.

His heart started to race.

Jamie must have felt it—his ears perked, his brows drawing together slightly as he placed a warm paw over Ryan's chest. "Hey," he murmured, concern flickering in his golden eyes. "Are you okay?"

Ryan's breath caught in his throat.

He wanted to say it. *Needed* to say it.

But those words were so heavy, so *dangerous*.

What if it was too soon? What if it changed everything?

Jamie studied him closely, his paw still resting against Ryan's chest, feeling every erratic beat of his heart.

Ryan swallowed hard, blinking away the moisture suddenly welling in his eyes. His lips trembled slightly, and when he finally spoke, his voice cracked.

"My whole life has been..." he trailed off, struggling to find the words. His ears flicked back, his breath uneven. "It's been nothing but self-doubt. Shame. *Uncertainty*."

Jamie didn't move, didn't interrupt—he listened.

Ryan exhaled shakily. "But with you," he whispered, voice thick, "all of that melts away."

Jamie's expression softened, his own breath hitching slightly.

Ryan blinked as a single tear escaped, rolling down his cheek. His throat bobbed as he struggled, *fought* to get the words out.

"Jamie, I..." He swallowed, his ears burning, his pulse *pounding* beneath Jamie's touch.

But then, finally—

"I love you."

His voice wavered, but there was no hesitation in his words. No doubt.

Ryan let out a breath, a tear slipping past his muzzle as he gave a shaky smile.

"It's the one thing I've ever been sure about."

A silence settled between them, thick and heavy, but not in a bad way.

Ryan held his breath, watching Jamie's expression closely, his heart hammering so loudly in his chest he was sure Jamie could hear it.

Jamie's ears twitched, his golden eyes flickering with something unreadable before a slow, deep blush spread across his cheeks. He looked down, his tail giving the tiniest flick behind him, as if trying to process what had just been said.

Ryan swallowed, anxiety creeping in, but before he could say anything, Jamie finally lifted his gaze again, meeting Ryan's eyes with something soft. Something sure.

A shy, genuine smile tugged at his lips.

"I love you too," Jamie murmured.

Ryan felt his whole body freeze. His breath hitched. His heart stopped.

Then, before he could even react, Jamie leaned in, his paws finding Ryan's cheeks as he kissed him—slow and deep, filled with feeling.

Ryan let out a soft noise of surprise before immediately melting into it, his paws sliding around Jamie's waist, pulling him close, pressing their bodies together once more.

Jamie sighed against his lips, tilting his head, deepening the kiss as his paws slid down Ryan's chest, lingering, exploring.

Ryan growled lowly, rolling Jamie onto his back as their kiss turned hungrier, more desperate. Jamie let out a small gasp, fingers tightening against Ryan's fur, his tail curling around Ryan's leg as they shifted and tangled together.

Ryan's body burned, the warmth of Jamie beneath him, the way Jamie sighed into his mouth, the way his fingers gripped and pulled—it sent electricity down his spine.

It didn't take long before things escalated again.

Round two was inevitable.

Chapter 14

The months that followed were nothing short of bliss. Dating turned into Jamie staying over more nights than not, and soon after, staying turned into moving in. Their lives meshed seamlessly—like they had always been meant to fit together.

Ryan would come home from work to find Jamie curled up on the couch, controller in hand, his eyes narrowed in deep concentration as he maneuvered through whatever game had his attention that week. Max would be sprawled lazily across Jamie's lap, looking up only to wag his tail as Ryan entered.

And, of course, Ryan *always* took the opportunity to be a menace.

"Hey, babe," Ryan cooed as he walked in one evening, tossing his gym bag to the side before creeping up behind Jamie.

Jamie barely spared him a glance, ears flicking. "Hey."

Ryan grinned, leaning right next to Jamie's ear. "Wow, you died fast."

Jamie flinched, his entire body tensing as his character let out a dramatic death cry on screen. His tail bristled. "RYAN."

Ryan threw his head back in laughter, dodging the weak swipe Jamie sent his way.

"You suck," Jamie muttered, furiously respawning.

"You love me," Ryan teased, leaning over the couch to kiss the top of Jamie's head.

Jamie rolled his eyes but smirked. "Yeah, yeah."

And he did.

He always would love him.

Ryan made sure of it.

No matter how much time passed, Ryan always checked in, always asked Jamie if he was okay, always reassured him, always held him a little too long when they hugged.

And Jamie? Jamie never failed to roll his eyes fondly, reach up, and flick Ryan's ear.

"I'm happy," he would say, firm and certain. "I'm so happy, Ryan."

And Ryan believed him.

Months had passed, and the two only grew more comfortable with one another.

Ryan stood at the kitchen counter, sorting through mail, tossing aside flyers and bills, when something caught his eye.

An envelope—thicker than the rest, sealed with elegant gold lettering.

He flipped it over.

It read:

Samuel & Ethan

Ryan's ears perked. "Jamie?" he called.

Jamie, who had been reclined on the couch with Max sprawled over him, hummed in response.

Ryan smirked. "We got invited to a wedding."

Jamie groaned. "Do I have to dress up?"

Ryan snorted, walking over and tossing the invitation onto Jamie's chest. "It's Sam's wedding."

Jamie blinked. His golden eyes flickered with realization, then softened. "Oh," he murmured. He sat up, scanning the invitation before looking up at Ryan with a small, teasing smile. "Guess we have to go, huh?"

Ryan grinned. "Damn right we do."

The magical day for Sam came swiftly.

The park was stunning.

Spring was in full bloom, the air crisp and cool, the scent of fresh flowers carried on the breeze. Vibrant petals lined the stone paths, weaving through lush green grass and towering trees that framed the ceremony space like something out of a fairy tale.

Ryan stood off to the side, adjusting his suit jacket, trying to ignore the way his nerves made his hands twitch.

Not because he was getting married—but because Sam was.

His best friend.

His first love.

His heart swelled as he glanced toward Sam, who stood just a few feet away, rolling his shoulders and smoothing down the front of his own suit.

Sam caught Ryan's gaze and let out a breathy chuckle. "You're looking at me like I'm about to pass out."

Ryan smirked. "*Are* you about to pass out?"

Sam huffed, shaking his head. "No." Then he paused. "... Maybe."

Ryan chuckled, stepping closer, lowering his voice. "Hey, it's your wedding. You get to feel however you want."

Sam exhaled, glancing toward the floral archway where his soon-to-be husband would soon appear. His ears flicked, his tail giving a single nervous twitch.

Ryan placed a steadying hand on his shoulder. "You're gonna be fine, man."

Sam turned to him, something fond flickering in his eyes.

"You know," he murmured, his voice quieter now, "you've come so far since we first worked together all that time ago."

His expression softened. "I don't think you realize how much it means to me that you're here."

Ryan's breath hitched slightly, emotion creeping up his throat.

Sam swallowed, blinking as he wiped at his eye with the sleeve of his jacket. "You'll always have a special place in my heart, Ryan."

Ryan clenched his jaw, his ears lowering slightly, but a small smile tugged at his lips. "Shit, Sam, you're gonna make *me* cry now."

Sam chuckled, sniffling as he shook his head.

Ryan exhaled, gathering himself, then nudged Sam's shoulder playfully. "Look, it's my job to make sure you feel good today, alright? So, let's get you married before you turn into a blubbering mess."

Sam huffed a laugh, shaking his head. "Yeah, yeah."

Then Ryan's expression sobered slightly. He glanced at Sam, his tail swaying once behind him. "Hey...thank you."

Sam tilted his head. "For what?"

Ryan hesitated, then gave a small, almost bashful shrug.

"For helping me realize that it's okay to be who I am," Ryan said, voice thick with meaning. "That there was never anything wrong with me."

Sam stared at him, his own eyes glassy with emotion.

Then, in one smooth motion, he pulled Ryan into a tight hug.

Ryan immediately returned it, his tail wagging slightly as he clapped Sam on the back.

They stayed like that for a long moment—two people who had once held so much unresolved tension, so many unspoken words—finally at peace.

When they finally pulled back, Ryan exhaled, rolling his shoulders.

"You ready?" he asked.

Sam let out a slow breath, then nodded, smiling.

"Yeah," he said. "I'm ready."

Ryan grinned.

And together, they turned toward the aisle—toward the future—watching as Sam's husband-to-be stepped forward, waiting at the altar.

The wedding was a blast.

The food was insanely good—beautifully plated dishes that tasted even better than they looked. Drinks flowed freely, laughter and conversation filled the air, and everyone seemed genuinely happy.

Ryan had barely gotten a moment to sit down, constantly pulled between different conversations, hugs, and teasing remarks from friends. But as the night went on, he found himself standing off to the side, sipping his drink and watching the dance floor.

And that's when he saw *them.*

Lysander and Bandaid.

The two of them were *close*, their bodies just barely brushing as they moved in sync to the music. Bandaid's usual playful grin softened into something almost mischievous, his tail flicking in excitement.

Ryan narrowed his eyes slightly.

Then—

Bandaid gave *the look.*

Ryan smirked, immediately recognizing the sly glint in Bandaid's eyes as he leaned in close to whisper something to Lysander. Lysander, ever composed, ever proper—immediately turned crimson. His tail fluffed slightly, and he tried to maintain his usual stoic expression, but Ryan saw the way his ears twitched, how his fingers curled slightly against Bandaid's wrist as he tugged him toward the wooded area nearby.

Ryan laughed, rolling his eyes as Bandaid practically dragged Lysander away from the crowd.

"They're *ridiculous*," he muttered to himself, shaking his head.

"They're an unlikely but perfect pair, aren't they?"

Ryan turned slightly, surprised to find Jamie standing beside him, watching the same scene unfold.

Jamie's golden eyes were soft, his tail swaying gently behind him, his ears twitching slightly in amusement.

Ryan chuckled, glancing back at the retreating duo. "Yeah. Yeah, they really are."

Then, the music shifted.

The upbeat tempo faded, replaced with something slow, something gentle.

Ryan felt Jamie's fingers brush against his.

He turned his head, meeting Jamie's gaze—warm, open, inviting.

Ryan exhaled, setting his drink aside. "May I have this dance?" he asked, grinning.

Jamie rolled his eyes but took Ryan's outstretched paw anyway. "I guess," he said, pretending to be reluctant. But the way his tail flicked excitedly gave him away.

Ryan pulled him close.

The world faded.

Under the moonlight, they moved together, slow and easy. Jamie's head rested against Ryan's chest, their bodies swaying in perfect time.

Ryan let his chin rest on top of Jamie's head, inhaling his familiar scent, feeling the steady rhythm of Jamie's heartbeat against him.

The soft glow of fairy lights twinkled around them, but the moon—*God, the moon*—was full and luminous above them, bathing them in silver light. Their shadows danced along the grass, moving as one.

Jamie's arms tightened around Ryan's waist, his body fitting so perfectly against his own.

Ryan closed his eyes, savoring the moment, the feel of Jamie in his arms, the realization that *this*—this was what happiness felt like.

It wasn't grand gestures. It wasn't over-the-top romance.

It was *this*.

Holding Jamie under the moonlight, with nothing but music and love surrounding them.

For the first time in his life, Ryan truly felt like he was floating.

The morning air was crisp, the scent of dew and earth fresh beneath Ryan's paws as he stepped carefully around the bed, making sure not to wake Jamie.

Jamie was still wrapped up in the blankets, his face buried in the pillow, his ears twitching slightly as he murmured something incoherent in his sleep. His tail was curled lazily behind him, his body completely at ease—safe, finally a sense of *home*.

Ryan paused for a moment, just watching him.

His heart squeezed.

Then, with a soft smile, he leaned down, pressing a featherlight kiss to Jamie's forehead before slipping out of the room.

Max padded beside him as they made their way down the quiet morning streets, his golden coat glowing slightly under the rising sun. The city was still waking up, the air cool against Ryan's fur, a gentle breeze stirring through the trees.

His usual route led him straight to the little café where he and Jamie had first met outside of the daycare.

Ryan stopped in front of the building, stepping to the side and peering through the window.

And there it was. *Their* table.

The memory played out in his mind—him fumbling with the bag, Jamie's face twisting in confusion, the accidental implication that had left Ryan a flustered mess. He chuckled softly, shaking his head.

God, if only he had known then.

If only he had known that the quiet, reserved, beautiful boy sitting across from him that day would be *everything*.

Ryan took a deep breath, stepping inside and ordering his usual coffee. As he waited, his thoughts drifted—back to the wedding, back to the way Sam had looked at his husband, back to the certainty in his eyes.

Love isn't just something that makes sense.

No—love, the truest love, *doesn't* always make sense.

It defies logic. It isn't about reason or careful planning.

It's that inexplicable knowing. That moment where you look at someone, and you don't have to think. You don't have to calculate. You don't need to question.

You just know.

Ryan knew it when Jamie blushed at his teasing.

He knew it when Jamie curled into him every night, his breath soft and even, completely trusting in Ryan's arms.

He knew it when Jamie, for all his guarded nature, had fought for him—not just physically, but emotionally, letting himself open up, letting himself be loved.

And Ryan knew it now, standing here, holding a warm coffee cup in his paws, feeling his heart pull toward the person still fast asleep in their bed.

He looked down at Max, who was sitting patiently at his side, his golden tail wagging lightly.

Ryan smirked, reaching down to scratch behind his ears.

"So," he murmured, his voice warm, playful. "How do you feel about tuxes, buddy?"

Max tilted his head, huffing softly, before nudging Ryan's leg with his nose.

Ryan chuckled, looking back toward the café window one last time before turning on his heel.

He had somewhere to be.

He had someone to get home to.

The evening was perfect.

Ryan and Jamie had gone to dinner, sharing soft laughter over their plates, sneaking bites from each other's meals, and letting the warm atmosphere settle between them like a well-worn embrace.

And then, as they often did, they walked.

The park stretched wide around them, the golden hues of the setting sun casting long, soft shadows. The air was cool, but not cold, carrying the distant scent of blooming flowers and fresh earth.

Ryan, as always, carried the conversation.

He told stories—little ones, silly ones, some exaggerated just to make Jamie roll his eyes and smirk. He talked about work, about Max, about Bandaid and Lysander and how blatantly obvious they were now.

Jamie listened, nodding along, offering small hums of acknowledgment and the occasional soft chuckle. But something about him felt…*off*.

Jamie was always quiet, but tonight, it was different.

Ryan could *feel* it—the slight hesitations, the way Jamie's ears twitched but didn't fully perk, the small pauses before he answered.

Maybe it was the wedding. Maybe Jamie was thinking about something bigger.

Maybe he knew.

Ryan's heart squeezed.

He tried to carry on, to push through the second-guessing thoughts, to *not* let his nerves show.

They continued up the hill, the incline slow and steady, their steps in sync. Ryan let out a slow breath, the warmth of the setting sun pressing against his fur as they finally reached the top.

And when he looked out at the horizon, something settled inside him.

The sky was painted in gold and lavender, streaked with

the last hints of daylight, a masterpiece only nature could create. Ryan's fingers twitched.

This was it.

This was the moment.

He turned, inhaling sharply, his pulse racing as he prepared to be brave—to be fearless, despite the way his heart pounded in his chest.

But—

He froze.

Because when he turned, Jamie wasn't standing.

He was *kneeling*.

His head was tilted downward, his paws trembling slightly, his shoulders shaking.

Tears streaked down his cheeks.

Ryan's stomach dropped. Panic flared in his chest. "Jamie—are you hurt? What's wrong?" He reached forward instinctively, but Jamie let out a soft, watery chuckle and shook his head.

And then—Jamie spoke.

"Ryan..." His voice wavered, thick with emotion. "You saved me."

Ryan stilled.

Jamie took a shaky breath, lifting his golden eyes, shimmering with tears but full of love.

"You found me when I had nothing left to give," he continued, his voice raw but sure. "When I was broken, when I had nearly given up on the idea of love." He swallowed, his ears twitching, his tail curling slightly behind him. "After Zack... after everything, I told myself I'd never do this again. That relationships, love, forever—it just wasn't for me."

Ryan's breath caught in his throat.

Jamie gave a tearful, trembling smile. "And then...*you* stumbled in the door."

Ryan felt his own eyes start to burn, his chest tight, his pulse erratic.

"You showed me what love was, Ryan," Jamie whispered. "You took someone like me—someone guarded, someone afraid—and made me feel like I was a treasure." His ears flicked, his gaze unwavering. "You make me feel like I'm worth everything."

Ryan's throat bobbed, his breath shuddering.

Jamie let out a quiet, breathy laugh, wiping at his tears with his wrist. "I know I'm not good with words," he admitted. "I know I'm not the most talkative hyena. I hide a lot of my feelings, I get in my own way." His voice dropped to something softer. "But last night...I saw Sam and his husband, and I wanted *that*."

Jamie exhaled shakily, his fingers clutching at the velvet box in his paw. "I saw them, and I knew." He blinked up at Ryan, his gaze filled with something deeper than words could ever express.

"I *need* you to know that I want you. Forever." His voice cracked slightly, but it never wavered.

Ryan sucked in a sharp breath, his vision blurring.

"You are my deep breath, Ryan." Jamie's lips trembled, but his smile remained. "You are my missing piece."

Then Jamie raised his paw and held out a ring.

Ryan *broke.*

A soft sob left him as he let out a laugh, covering his mouth with his paw, his whole body shaking. He reached into his pocket and took out his own ring.

Jamie smiled, his tail flicking slightly. "I take this is a mutual thing then?"

Ryan tackled Jamie, wrapping his arms so tightly around him that Jamie let out a small grunt, laughing through his tears. Ryan's muzzle pressed against Jamie's neck, his whole body trembling as he nodded against his fur.

"Yes," Ryan finally choked out. "God, yes."

Jamie laughed again, breathless, pressing his forehead

against Ryan's.

The sun dipped below the horizon, casting them in the soft glow of twilight, their shadows intertwined as one. Ryan knew at last where his place was. It was here, with the person who he knew he could trust with what was most important after all of the hardships.

The rest of his heart.

Ryan

Jamie

Sam

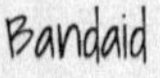

Bandaid

Lysander

www.ingramcontent.com/pod-product-compliance
Lightning Source LLC
LaVergne TN
LVHW090940080826
845145LV00003B/826

* 9 7 8 1 6 2 4 7 5 2 8 5 8 *